# SCOTT MCCULLY

Espionage ( 1 ) Adventure

# A
# TRAGIC
# INTRODUCTION

By

Jessica C. Jo

D1506453

A TRAGIC INTRODUCTION

International Standard Book Number: 978-1-981-09959-7

Cover design by Elijah Principe

Printed in the United States of America

For more information:

Jessica C. Joiner

jcjauthor@gmail.com

https://authorjessicajoiner.weebly.com

## Other Books By Jessica C. Joiner

### Scott McCully Espionage Adventures

(1) A Tragic Introduction
(2) Vengeance Is Mine
(3) Deadly Secrets
(4) Escape Into Certain Doom
(5) Loyal to the End

### As a Sword in My Bones

# Chapter

Hike!

I caught the snap and dropped back. Holding the football ready, I scanned the field for an open receiver. It was the first game of my senior season, we were up twenty-one to three, and I was looking for my fourth touchdown pass of the game. Our rivals, the Northern Peak Prep Soaring Eagles, had struggled to break our line all game, leaving me free to run nearly any play in the Minuteman handbook without fear.

I risked a glance into the stands, but still couldn't see my parents. Usually at least Mom made a point to be at my games. I shook my head and brought my focus back to the play. Things probably just got out of hand at work. It seemed to happen more frequently lately.

My wide receiver spun free of his opponent and headed toward the end zone. I hurled my arm forward, sending the ball spiraling into the air.

Crunch!

Something hard hit me in the chest, caught my face mask, and snapped my head back. I was on the ground before I could react, struggling to catch the breath that had been knocked out of me while the field tipped crazily. Pulling off my helmet, I rolled to my side, spit out my mouth guard, and sucked in a ragged breath. The crowd was eerily silent.

"Scott!" Matt Marshall, my best friend and star linebacker, knelt beside me and laid his hand on my back. "Are you all right?"

"I'm fine." I tried to push myself up to sitting, but my head throbbed and my neck ached. "Help me up before Coach gets here. I need to get back to the game."

"You're not going back to the game." Coach Shiloah crouched in front of me and his daughter Trinity stood behind him. Both were looking at me worriedly. Coach Shiloah waved his hand in front of my face. "Eyes on me, Cadet McCully. That was a bad hit. Do you hurt anywhere?"

It was really tempting to lie so I could go back to the game. "My head and neck hurt," I said with a sigh. With Coach Shiloah's help I finally managed to sit up. "What hit me?"

# A Tragic Introduction

"A little weasel on the other team hit you high after you threw the ball." Matt glared and scanned the group of players circled curiously around us.

"Cadet Marshall." Coach Shiloah's voice held a note of warning. "Help me get Scott to the bench. He needs Dr. Grant to take a look at him."

Matt hesitated, his eyes still on the crowd. Well, one member of it anyway. A wiry teen in a white and green Soaring Eagles uniform smirked back at him.

"Nice play, you little jerk." Matt clenched his fists and stepped toward the opposing player. "This is football, not WWE."

"Quarterbacks get hit." The smaller teen shrugged and sneered at Matt. "It's part of the game. Perhaps if you had been guarding him better, this wouldn't have happened."

"Don't let him get to you, Matt." I tried to take a wobbly step toward them, but Coach Shiloah held me back.

"He certainly let *me* get to *you*," the mouthy teen called. His teammates snickered behind him. "Thanks for handing us the win, Marshall."

With a roar of rage, Matt rushed the laughing teen, driving him to the grass in the middle of the crowd. Players from both sides shouted and began pushing each other. The benches for both teams emptied as coaches and refs ran to pull the brawling players apart.

# Jessica C. Joiner

"Break it up!" Coach Shiloah yelled. He didn't let go of me or move any closer to the fight, so the rest of the students ignored him.

A pair of men jogged past us into the fight. Richard Hinkly, a slim, gray haired man in a blue pinstriped suit and red tie, was the Superintendent of John Jay Military Academy. The other man, an athletic twenty-something wearing a black suit over a black turtleneck, was Matt's older brother Chris.

"Cadets, attention!" Superintendent Hinkly commanded, his voice clear and crisp. Blue uniforms separated from white and green, scrambled to attention, and saluted. "Cadet Marshall, your behavior is unbecoming to a member of this school."

"Sir, I'm sorry, sir." Matt's apology didn't reach his defiant expression. His jersey was askew, grass stained his pants, and one of his scowling brown eyes was beginning to blacken. "But that guy hit Cadet McCully high." He looked to his brother for support. "The little jerk wanted Scott out of the game."

Chris frowned, his sharp eyes taking in Matt's condition, but didn't respond. Instead he just looked over at me. His frown deepened and something hardened in his expression.

"There will be no excuses, Cadet," Superintendent Hinkly told Matt. "You're done for today. Hit the showers."

"Sir, yes, sir." Matt saluted stiffly, threw a final glare at his enemy on the other team, and stomped off

# A Tragic Introduction

toward the locker room, scooping his helmet up off the ground as he passed me.

"The rest of you take your places," Superintendent Hinkly ordered. "Dismissed."

He turned to me. His face – famous among the students for its limited range of one "Stone-faced" expression – was sympathetic. The change made me uncomfortable. I hadn't been hit *that* hard.

"Unfortunately, you're also out for the game, Cadet McCully," he said. "You've been hurt and Agent Marshall has an urgent matter to discuss with you."

"I'll take care of Scott, Coach," Matt's brother offered. His voice was soft as as he stepped to my side. "Your team needs you and I need a few words with him."

"I'm good, really," I protested, taking a tentative step away from Coach Shiloah's supporting arm to prove it. "Just a headache, that's all."

*Why would Matt's brother want to talk to me?* Chris had basically been Matt's mom and dad since their mother had passed away and their father had buried himself in his military career. His job in law enforcement took him away for weeks at a time, but he still managed to make time for Matt when he was around. His being here wasn't odd. His specifically needing to speak to me was.

"Take him by the bench to see the team doctor," Coach Shiloh ordered. "Then he's all yours."

# Jessica C. Joiner

An impatient look crossed Chris's face, but he nodded tightly. He gave me the same assessing look he'd given Matt. "Headache?"

"Just a headache," I insisted as I picked up my helmet on our way off the field. "He caught me off guard and knocked the wind out of me."

"Double vision? Dizziness? Nausea?" Chris crossed his arms over his chest and watched me critically as I sat on the bench and Dr. Grant started his exam.

"No, no, and no. I've been playing football since I was nine. I know what a concussion feels like." I chuckled and teased, "You sound like my mom."

A grim look I'd never seen before crossed Chris's face. Fear sent an icy spike down my spine.

"Why are you here, exactly?" I asked him slowly. "Matt didn't mention that he was spending the weekend with you."

Chris fingered a pair of dark glasses that hung from the breast pocket of his suit coat. "I didn't come to see Matt." He looked back to the doctor. "How is he, doc? I'm going to need to steal him away for a minute."

"I don't see any signs of a concussion." Dr. Grant shook his head. "Keep an eye on him for the next few hours. If he complains of any new symptoms, get him checked out immediately."

"I told you I was fine." My heart was beginning to pound. Chris was in law enforcement. My parents didn't make the game. Two and two added up to a very

## A Tragic Introduction

frightening conclusion. *Lord, please let them be okay.* "Is this about why my parents didn't show up for the game?"

A muscle tensed in Chris's jaw as he pulled the sunglasses from his pocket and put them on. Not a very reassuring sign.

"Superintendent Hinkly gave permission for us to use his office." Chris turned to leave the stadium. "Get changed and meet me there."

I nodded and swallowed back my fear. "Chris? Can Matt come along?"

Chris turned back to look at me, the dark glasses masking his expression. He sighed. "I think that actually would be a good idea."

For a moment I stood rooted to the sidelines, then I dashed into the locker rooms. The thought that something terrible had happened to my parents and Matt's brother had somehow been given the responsibility to break the news to me made me run faster than I'd ever rushed for a touch down. I tossed my helmet on a bench and yanked my jersey over my head without even breaking stride.

"Matt, hurry up," I shouted at the only running shower as I tore open my locker and started to throw on my Academy uniform. "Your brother says he needs to talk, and I –" My voice caught. "I have a feeling it's not good."

The water cut off and Matt stuck his head out of the shower. "Give me a minute to get dressed."

Now I *was* nauseous, but not from a head injury. I rubbed on a thick layer of deodorant to make up for the fact that I wasn't going to take time to shower. Chris normally had a cool, easy going manner that contrasted Matt's passion and quick temper. None of that was here today. I threw my normal meticulous attention to detail out the window, glancing in a mirror only long enough to make sure I wasn't going to be begging for demerits when I stepped outside. I passed a hand over my short, blond hair to smooth it down, fear reflecting back at me in my blue eyes. It was like looking at a younger version of my dad, from my blond hair to my slim, six foot tall frame. The blue eyes came from my mom.

*Please let them be all right.* I turned from the mirror. If someone wanted to give me demerits for being out of uniform, they could take it up with Superintendent Hinkly. I was willing to bet the compassionate look he'd given me earlier meant he knew what Chris was here for.

*Knew and felt pity for me.* My stomach twisted. *Lord, how bad is it really?*

"I'm ready," Matt announced, raking his fingers though his brown hair instead of using a comb. His worried look met my eyes. "Whatever it is, God has it under control, you know that."

I did, but knowing and feeling were entirely different things. And right now things felt very much out of control.

We quickly made our way across campus to the Nathan Hale Administration building. With everyone at the game, the halls were empty. Even the secretary that usually sat in the waiting room to Superintendent Hinkly's office was gone for the day.

# A Tragic Introduction

"There's Chris." Matt nudged my arm and pointed at the open door to the office. Chris sat perched on the corner of Superintendent Hinkly's desk tapping his sunglasses against his leg.

His red-rimmed eyes and tight lips made my stomach clench again.

"How bad is it?" I asked bluntly as Matt closed the door behind us. "I know it's bad: even Superintendent Hinkly looked sorry for me."

"Take a seat." Chris gestured to a pair of chairs facing the desk and his suit coat fell open, revealing a hand gun in a shoulder holster like detectives wore on TV.

Clenching my teeth against the panic welling up inside me, I did as I was told. The gun only confirmed what I already knew. Chris was here on business, not a social call.

He blew out a slow breath, as if steeling himself for what he was about to say. "Scott, there's no easy way to tell you this, but I thought it would be better coming from someone you know."

*Just say it!* I wanted to scream at him. I gripped the arms of my chair so tightly my fingernails bit into the wood.

"Your parents' plane crashed not far from here early yesterday morning." Chris paused as if looking for the right words and his gaze dropped to the sunglasses in his hands. His voice trembled and lowered. "I'm afraid there were no survivors."

# Chapter

*I didn't hear him right. Surely I couldn't have heard him right.* My chest tightened as if someone was trying to squeeze the life out of me. I swallowed hard, forcing down the lump in my throat that threatened to gag me. *This can't be happening. It's a nightmare – some cruel joke. It has to be!*

"We're doing everything we can to find out how the crash happened." Chris's voice pushed its way into my thoughts, sounding miles away. I stared at him blankly. "As soon as we know anything, I'll let you know."

"Are you sure they're…" Matt trailed off. His voice was husky with emotion.

I vaguely noticed a horrified look on Matt's face as I tried to force myself back to reality, a reality I wasn't sure I was ready to face.

"As sure as we can be." Chris put his sunglasses on, hiding his own moist eyes, but his weak voice betrayed him. You'd have thought his parents had been the ones to die. "I can't give you any details, but I wouldn't be here if we weren't sure."

*How could you let this happen, Lord?* I'd expected bad news, but this was even worse than I'd feared. Both of them, gone? I wanted to get up and run out of the room, but I felt glued to the seat.

Chris cleared his throat and stood. His hands were tight fists at his sides. "You can't possibly understand how sorry I am. If you need anything, just call. Matt knows how to reach me."

I sat, staring straight ahead, until Chris had closed the door behind him, trying to sort out the mess of facts and emotions that swirled through my brain.

"They're not dead," I whispered, as my thoughts cleared. "They can't be." I refused to accept it. Chris was wrong. He had to be wrong.

"Scott," Matt said softly. He laid his hand on my arm. Matt was tough, but his mom had died when he was younger and I knew he understood. "I'm sorry. If there's anything I can do…"

# A Tragic Introduction

"I just need to go to my room to think." I shook my throbbing head and pushed myself out of the chair. Things just didn't make sense. "Chris isn't telling me everything."

"Are you suggesting he lied to you?" Matt asked, his eyes darkening angrily.

"No! I'm just… I don't know." I broke off in frustration. I didn't need an argument with my best friend on top of everything else. "Look, I'm sorry. I just need to think things through, all right? It's a lot to take in."

"Believe me, I know," Matt said, compassion replacing his quick anger.

We left Superintendent Hinkly's office and walked back through the waiting room silently. Each of us was too absorbed in his own thoughts to speak.

*What were my parents doing in town?* I pushed open the door leading to the hall, only partly paying attention to what I was doing. *Did they crash coming to see me?* That thought just made me feel guilty. *And why on earth would Chris be so upset about their crash? Surely as an FBI agent or whatever he is he's gotten used to breaking bad news to people.*

"Oh!" a girl yelped in front of me. "Hey, watch the door."

"Sorry, Trinity," I apologized, blushing.

Trinity Shiloh was a pretty blue-eyed junior with wavy, shoulder-length red hair always pulled back into a ponytail. She was the coach's daughter and another close friend, but she could still made me feel awkward.

"Is the game over?" I stammered, looking for something to say. "Did we win?"

She looked away, uncomfortably playing with a locket her dad had given her for her tenth birthday. "Nah. Not without you two." She lifted her blue eyes to my face, concern still reflected in them. "Are you okay? That tackle looked awful."

I gave her a smooth smile. "Dr. Grant says I'm fine. Nothing to be worried about." *Except that my life has been turned upside down.* My smile faltered and my stomach turned again.

Trinity narrowed her eyes and put her hands on her hips. "What aren't you telling me, Scott?" She glared at Matt. "What's he not telling me?"

"He just found out…" Matt began.

"Some bad news about my family," I finished firmly. I didn't want to hear the whole thing all over again. I'd tell her later. "That's all."

"He found out his parents were apes," a high-pitched voice mocked behind us. "He's disappointed he couldn't rank Neanderthal."

The three of us turned to face a short teen with black hair spiked a little in the latest style wearing a pair of designer jeans and a tee shirt with the logo of an expensive teen clothing company advertised across the front. He looked familiar, but I couldn't quite place him.

"You!" Trinity recognized him immediately.

## A Tragic Introduction

"What are you doing here, cheater?" Matt snarled as he shoved past me. "You'd better have come to apologize for your rotten behavior at the game."

"Let it go, Matt." I rolled my eyes and sighed. Now I recognized the sneering teen that had hit me. I was in no mood to deal with him right now, or mediate a fight between him and Matt.

"Daytonas don't apologize," the spoiled little brat sniffed. A mean smile curled his lips. "Besides, we won, so I don't even see why I should."

With a low growl, Matt lunged for the teen, pulling up short when I stepped between them.

"I'm Scott McCully," I introduced myself and offered the kid my hand, determined to put the game behind us. "The offices are closed. Can I help you with something?"

"The name's Winston." The teen drew himself up to his full height and ignored my hand. "Winston Daytona the third. Of the Boston Daytonas. I'm here visiting your school."

"I don't care if you come from the NASCAR Daytonas," Matt snapped, taking a step toward the smaller teen. "You can't just be rude to whoever you want."

"And you *do* owe Scott an apology," Trinity added. "You could have really hurt him out there."

"Forget it." I placed my hand on Matt's shoulder. Winston was an annoying jerk, but all I really wanted was the privacy of my own room. "Let's just go."

# Jessica C. Joiner

"What's the matter?" Winston stood on his tiptoes to get up in Matt's face. "Neanderthal boy need to keep you from doing something you'll regret?"

"I already regret having met you," Matt seethed, turning with some effort to follow me. "I'd better go before I make you regret having met *me*."

"Sure go," Winston taunted as the three of us walked away from him. "You haven't seen the last of me."

"Ugh," Trinity groaned as we left the administration building. "I'm glad he doesn't come to our school. Can you imagine dealing with *that* every day?"

"It would take the patience of Job," Matt muttered glaring back at Winston.

Trinity raised an eyebrow and looked to me.

"From the Bible," I answered. "He was put through horrible trials, but his faith in God kept him from sin." I nudged Matt with my elbow. "You should have asked for the patience of Job before you rushed that jerk on the field."

Matt blushed. "Yeah. Sorry." Fire flared in his eyes, replacing the apology as he looked at me. "Nobody messes with my friends."

"I'll remember that, the next time I'm tempted to get my revenge when Scott strikes me out in softball," Trinity laughed as we reached the boys dorms. "In the meantime, perhaps you should read up on that Job guy. Sounds like you could learn a few things."

# A Tragic Introduction

Waving to her, Matt and I headed into the Alexander Hamilton boys' dorm. We climbed a flight of stairs and walked down the hall to our second floor dorm room. Our room was just the same as the rest of the rooms on our floor: two bunks, two dressers, and two desks. Nothing was allowed on the walls, so the only personal touch was a cork board above each desk that the students could decorate with pictures or posters.

As I swung the door open, my eyes rested on a picture of my parents and me tacked to my cork board. It was from a trip we had taken last summer. They were smiling out at me as if nothing could ever go wrong. As if we would always be a family. I snatched the picture off the cork board and laid it face down next to the computer on my desk. The reminder of my loss was more than I could bear to look at right now.

*Why, Lord? Why take them from me like this?* I crossed the room and tossed myself onto my bed while Matt closed the door. Trinity's teasing about Matt reading Job probably could apply just as easily to me right now. I could relate to his feelings of loss.

"It just doesn't make sense," I protested after a moment, staring blankly at the ceiling. "My parents weren't even supposed to *be* just outside town, they weren't supposed to get in until today."

"Maybe they came back early," Matt suggested. He pulled his chair away from his desk and straddled it, folding his arms across the back of the chair.

"Maybe," I said slowly. My thoughts were clearing, but things still didn't make sense. I rose to one elbow and turned to Matt. "But still, Dad's a great pilot. A careful pilot. Careful pilots don't just crash. Something made him crash."

"Chris said they were still investigating," Matt reminded me with a shrug.

"They? The FBI? FAA?" I asked, feeling a little exasperated. "Who does he work for anyway? He's never said."

"He doesn't really talk about it much," Matt answered slowly, as if he feared incriminating his brother. "He's in law enforcement. Some security group, I think, sort of like your parents' work for Global Security Services."

"Why would a security group be investigating a plane crash?" Things just weren't adding up. "Haven't you ever asked him where he works? Seriously, what kinds of conversations do you guys *have* at the dinner table?"

Matt flushed and I instantly regretted my words. Chris and Matt's dad had fought over Chris's career plans when he'd left for college. It was precisely the topic they would avoid most carefully.

"Sorry, Matt." I dropped back on the bed and threw my arm over my eyes. "That was out of line."

"No, you're right," Matt agreed reluctantly. "I guess his being involved *is* a little odd."

"More than a *little* odd," I clarified. "Chris isn't telling us everything."

"Maybe he doesn't *know* anything more," Matt pointed out, a little defensively.

## A Tragic Introduction

"Well, *someone* could have at least told me *something* before now." I sat up and tapped my chest for emphasis. "They're *my* parents. Besides, if they crashed just outside of town don't you think we'd have heard something on the news? Wouldn't a plane crash just outside Baltimore draw a little attention?"

"Normally," Matt agreed tiredly. "I don't know, Scott, maybe they tried to hush it up."

"Why?" I got up and paced the small room anxiously. "Why would anyone want to hush up a plane crash involving two normal citizens? Unless…"

"Unless what?" Matt sighed and shook his head slightly, as if he was beginning to see where this was headed and didn't like it.

I was pretty sure I didn't like it either.

"Unless my parents weren't really normal citizens." I stopped mid-stride and turned to face Matt.

"I've met your parents," Matt reminded me, looking as if he was thoroughly convinced I'd lost it. "They're not exactly the same kind of security guards as Chris. No offense, but the most danger your parents have ever faced is the risk of heat exhaustion at a baseball game. Do they even *carry* guns?

"You don't know them like I do." I crossed to my desk and picked up the picture I'd laid down. I turned it to Matt, pointing to a fading mark surrounding my dad's eye. "They're not normal. They're supposed to be the kind of security guards that protect paintings and famous people. Not the kind that get up and go on long trips at all hours of the night. Not the kind that come home from work looking like they've gone five rounds with George Foreman."

"Everybody has bad days." Matt responded weakly, uncertainty on his face as he looked at the photo.

"And Chris – you saw him – he was really upset." The more I thought about it, the more convinced I was that I was right. "More upset than just a friend giving bad news. It was personal to him. What if they worked *with* Chris?"

"Maybe Chris could tell you more." Matt didn't even sound like *he* believed it anymore.

"Like he did today?" I scoffed. "You heard him; he can't give us any details. We'll have to find out for ourselves."

"Right, because that's what any teen would do in our place," Matt said sarcastically. "Are you insane? If you're right, that's all the more reason to leave this to the pros!"

"Pros like Chris who can't – or won't – tell me what's going on?" My voice filled with determination as I clenched my fist and looked back at my parents' faces in the photo. "I have to know what happened to them. No matter what it takes."

# Chapter

Matt hesitated, then sighed. "What do you want to do?"

"I'm going to find that crash site." I slapped the photo back on my desk and headed for the door. "Someone had to see the plane go down. Chris and Global Security Services couldn't silence everyone."

"We need to go back down to Superintendent Hinkly's office and get passes," Matt reminded me, resignation in his voice.

"We?" Surprised by Matt's sudden agreement, I stopped with my hand on the doorknob and looked back at him. "Are you sure you want to come?"

"Of course." Matt stood up from the chair and smiled tightly. "You're my best friend; I'm not letting you do this alone. Besides, you've got me curious now."

When we returned to the reception room, we found Superintendent Hinkly there talking to his receptionist.

"I took the liberty of telling Sergeant Mason that you two were excused from evening formation, to give you a little time to yourself." A faint look of concern crossed Superintendent Hinkly's face. I was beginning to wish he would just go back to looking stern. "If you need time, I can also excuse you from the rest of your classes for the week."

A week off classes would allow me to investigate uninterrupted. It also might look suspicious if I wasn't using it to plan a funeral or something. "No thank you, sir. I think I'd like to stick close to my regular routine. I'd also rather that not everyone knew about what happened, at least not until my grandparents make arrangements."

The sudden thought of dozens of students and teachers offering their sympathy made my stomach clench, but the thought that my grandparents would have to be notified eventually was far worse. If I couldn't prove my parents were still alive fast, I would be planning that funeral after all. My knees weakened and I leaned on the desk for support, hoping they didn't notice. I cleared my throat. "There is one thing, sir."

## A Tragic Introduction

"Anything," Superintendent Hinkly agreed.

"I would like to go out for a while." It was unusual for a student to be allowed off campus on a Thursday, but I hoped Superintendent Hinkly would make an exception, considering the circumstances. "Me and Matt. We'll be back by curfew."

Superintendent Hinkly nodded as he quickly signed the necessary passes and handed them to me. He looked me in the eye as he continued. His face looked stern, but his eyes were full of sympathy. "I'm really sorry about your parents, Cadet."

I looked away sharply. Superintendent Hinkly's sympathy threatened to resurface the doubts I was trying to suppress. *Please don't let me be wrong.* "Thank you, sir," I managed, forcing myself to sound stronger than I felt.

As soon as we were dismissed, I turned and headed out of Superintendent Hinkly's office. I wanted to get out of there before I changed my mind about leaving.

Matt and I went straight to the parking lot. Few of the students had cars, and my battered, brown sedan stood out among the teachers' newer models.

A lump threatened to choke me again as we approached my car. It had been my dad's car before he'd bought a newer one. He had given it to me when I turned sixteen. He and Mom had promised to get me a new car when I graduated from the Academy, but now…

I shook my head. Everything seemed to remind me of my parents. I had to focus on finding them, not worry about what might have happened to them.

Pushing aside my fear, I climbed inside, waited for Matt to be seated, and drove to the gate. After we showed our passes to the student assigned to guard the gate, we pulled out onto the road.

"So, do you have a plan?" Matt looked at me with his arms crossed over his chest. "The Baltimore area is huge and 'not far from here' could mean anywhere between DC and Pennsylvania."

"True," I conceded as I pulled into traffic, "but I doubt even Chris could cover up a plane crash in the heart of Baltimore, or especially closer to the Capitol. We stick to the west suburbs today."

We drove a rough series of arcs further and further from the Academy asking every shop owner and gas station attendant we found if they had noticed a plane crash early the previous morning. No one had seen anything. Or would admit to having seen anything.

"If we don't find something soon, we'll need to head back," Matt commented finally, looking at his watch. "You know what'll happen if we miss curfew. I'm not really in the mood for three laps around the campus and fifty push-ups."

I bit back a sharp retort. I was willing to keep looking all night if I had to, push-ups or no push-ups, but I allowed reason to prevail. Even I was beginning to realize how long a shot this was. *Perhaps grilling Chris would be more profitable after all.* "One more stop." I sighed. "If we don't find out anything there, we'll head back for the night."

# A Tragic Introduction

We stopped at a small gas station edging the state park. The bell on the door tinkled as we entered the tiny convenience store. A heavy-set man stood behind the cluttered counter.

"Excuse me, sir," I began as we walked up to the counter. The front of the counter was lined with candy bars. Right now, even the thought of eating one made me sick. I focused instead on the man's name tag. It read "Walter."

"Do you young men want a fill-up?" Walter asked eagerly as he looked appreciatively at our crisp military-style uniforms.

"Uh, not today," I said, slightly amused by the man's eagerness. I felt a little bad about wasting the man's time, even if the gas station was empty at the moment. *We probably should buy something.* "We'll take some of these." I bent and grabbed a random pair of candy bars. Matt reached into a display case and added an energy drink to the pile. "Can we ask you a question while you ring those up?"

"I'll help if I can." Walter grinned, scanning the barcodes on the candy bars. "What is it you want to know?"

"We were wondering if you saw a plane crash early yesterday morning?" I asked. *Please let him say yes.*

"I'm not really supposed to talk about it." Walter hesitated. "The police said…"

"My parents were on that plane," I whispered as my voice threatened to crack.

"Wow, kid, I'm sorry." Walter's eyes went wide. "I did see it – couldn't miss it. Nearly crashed right into this building."

I caught Matt's excited glance out of the corner of my eye, but kept my attention on Walter.

"Did you see where it went?" I absently wiped my sweaty palms on my pants. Now we were getting somewhere!

"Yeah, it went down in the park." The man motioned behind him with his thumb. "I called the police right away."

"Can you show us the place the plane crashed?" Eagerness crept into my voice.

"I can't just leave the station." He looked shocked at the suggestion. "Turn left at the little side road just south of here. Just drive down the road and look for a police line. They roped off the entire area."

"Thank you, sir." I hurriedly paid him and turned to go. Matt grabbed the drink and candy bars off the counter. I had totally forgotten about them. "You've been a great help."

"Any time." Walter nodded.

"Odd that the press didn't find out about the crash," I commented to Matt as we drove down the road.

"Especially if the police were called in," Matt agreed as he popped open his drink can. He was beginning to catch my excitement. "Perhaps you were right about a cover up."

# A Tragic Introduction

"We'll have to hurry if we're going to find anything." I glanced out the window. The sky glowed a deep orange as the sun began to sink below the horizon. *Please, Lord, help us find it before dark.*

We turned down a barely marked road that ran right into the state park. I would never have thought to turn down that particular road on my own. After that, the crash site was easy to find. A bright yellow police line marked off a large section of the woods along the right shoulder of the road. I thanked God for leading us there as I pulled the car off the road and looked around for Chris or police officers. There was nobody in sight.

"I guess they must be finished," Matt commented, tossing his empty can on the floor of my car. I was too focused on the chance to find out what really happened to my parents to chastise him now.

"They probably waited until they were finished to come tell me anything," I reasoned sourly as I ducked under the police line with Matt close behind.

"It doesn't take a pro to see where the plane went down," Matt said, pointing to broken branches and saplings as we walked. Further ahead, a gash was torn into the ground where the plane had plowed into the underbrush.

I didn't answer.

"You okay with this?" Matt picked his way to my side over a patch of poison ivy. "We still could leave it up to Chris."

# Jessica C. Joiner

"No," I said softly. My throat felt tight as I turned to look Matt in the eye. "If Chris and GSS have their way, I'll never know what really happened to my parents. I have to do this."

Matt paused as if debating whether to say more. Blowing a slow breath through his lips, he plunged ahead. "Scott, what if it really is like Chris said? What if we find… what if they're…"

I held up my hand to stop him. I wasn't going to think about that possibility. I *refused* to think about it. *They're not dead!* My voice wavered a bit as I tried to say firmly, "I have to know what happened – who they really were. Even if they are…" I couldn't bring myself to say the word "dead." It was as if saying the word was admitting it was a possibility. "Well, I need to know what happened. If Chris can't or won't tell me what I need to know, I'll have to find out for myself."

Determinedly, I stepped over a large tree limb and down into the groove made in the ground down the trail made by the plane. I'd only gone a few steps when I saw something familiar on the ground. My stomach tightened anxiously as I knelt to pick up my Dad's favorite pair of sunglasses. I had always teased him that they made him look like a secret agent. It was just a joke, but now they just reminded me that there was more to my parents than I knew. I swallowed hard as I stared at them. The sight of something that actually connected my parents to this crash made it seem more real and less like a nightmare or a bad television show.

# A Tragic Introduction

"Scott…"Matt stepped over an overturned stone and laid a hand on my shoulder.

I stuffed the glasses into my pocket without a word and continued down the trail. I hadn't really anticipated how hard visiting the crash site was going to be when I had decided to do it, but I wasn't going to let a pair of sunglasses stop me now.

My breath caught in my throat. Right ahead of us was the barely recognizable form of an airplane. Its name, *The Spook,* was clearly painted on one of the crumpled sides. Dad had named it for it's smoky-white color, but now it's name took on a double meaning. Panic made my heart pound inside me. I had hoped that I'd find out that it wasn't his, that, after all, my parents' deaths had been just a horrible mistake. It was horrible all right, a horrible reality. I felt like I was going to be sick. My heart raced and my knees threatened to give out beneath me. Maybe I would be better off letting Chris investigate, like a normal person.

"Let's go back to the car," Matt suggested. Even he was unable to take his eyes off the tragic scene. "This was a bad idea."

"No," I forced out, my voice husky. I took a breath and steadied myself. I'd come this far; I was going to follow through.

I nervously made my way over to the plane, very tempted to take Matt's advice and turn around. *Lord, help me to be right.* Desperation filled me and I blinked rapidly to fight off the tears stinging my eyes. *Please make my parents be okay.*

# Jessica C. Joiner

There was no doubt it was Dad's plane, as far as I could tell by what was left of it, which wasn't much. One of the wings and part of the pilot's side of the plane had been blown off and scorch marks darkened the side. The crash hadn't been an accident. Only a bomb or something similar would have caused that kind of damage. Bile rose in my mouth as I realized that someone had tried to kill my parents.

With a gulp and a shake of my head, I examined the wreckage. The plane had slammed into a large oak tree, folding the front of the plane like an accordion until the control panel nearly touched the pilot's seat. My knees buckled and I leaned against the broken remaining wing to steady myself. There was no way anyone inside could have survived that crash. I willed myself to go further to look inside the destroyed cabin.

*My parents aren't dead, and I'm going to prove it.*

"There's no blood," I muttered as I stuck my head further into the wreckage.

"What are you doing?" Matt drew closer and leaned into the opening.

"There's no blood." I pulled my head out of the plane and turned to Matt. "If my parents had been in this plane when it crashed, there would be a lot of blood."

"That's morbid, Scott." Matt frowned at me. "This isn't a movie."

"Maybe, but it's true." Relief made me feel giddy. "Chris never said that they had found any bodies."

# A Tragic Introduction

"I think that was assumed." Matt's eyes were wide.

"What if he didn't say it because they haven't found any? My parents could have bailed out just before the crash. They could still be alive!" My voice rose excitedly.

"Don't jump to conclusions," Matt warned gently. "Chris wouldn't have said anything unless they were very sure."

"I'm going to see if there's anything else in the plane." I ignored Matt as I leaned back inside. "Maybe I can find out why they were back in town."

"Hurry up," Matt urged anxiously. "It's getting dark."

"I won't be much longer." Squeezing in deeper, I scraped my leg against the mangled passenger seat. I took a sharp breath and bit my lip against the pain, but continued looking. There wasn't much in the plane, not even personal belongings. I'd have thought my parents would have at least had a suitcase. Chris and the police seemed to have gone over it pretty well.

*Still, maybe they missed something.* I squeezed into the cockpit and stuck my arm between pilot's seat and the smashed controls. It was a tight fit, but I could now reach under the seat to feel if anything had slid underneath during the crash, something that could have been missed. My fingers closed on a small slip of paper.

## Jessica C. Joiner

"I found something!" I called excitedly, struggling to free my arm without letting go of the paper. "Help me out."

"What did you find?" Matt asked, allowing a little curiosity into his voice as he pulled me out of the wreck.

"This piece of paper was under the pilot's seat. I could barely reach it." I held the paper close to my face to read it in the failing sunlight: "'Contact: Hayes.' There's a phone number here."

"Hayes?" Matt asked. "Who's Hayes?"

"I don't know. Maybe Mom and Dad were going to meet him," I said and added to myself, *or maybe he tried to kill them.* "Anyway it's a clue."

"Which we'll investigate tomorrow. It's getting late. We have to get back." Matt turned back down the path the way we came.

"I guess you're right." I sighed. I wanted to check the phone number as soon as possible, but I couldn't risk drawing attention to what we were doing. Not now. "Let's go."

As I turned to follow Matt, I noticed something on the ground glittering in the last rays of sunset. It was hidden under a fallen tree limb. The angle of the sunlight had just been able to reach it. I bent to pick it up and looked at it carefully. It was a silver plastic card with raised numbers on it and a textured silver image of the planet Saturn, but no words. I stuffed it into my back pocket, promised myself that I would ask Chris about it later, and ran to catch up with Matt.

# A Tragic Introduction

It was barely ten minutes before curfew when we got back to the Academy. I parked the car, and we headed toward the boys' dorms. Matt had tried to start a conversation on the way back, but I had been too preoccupied with my own thoughts to talk. We were still silent as we mounted the concrete steps leading up to the three story Hamilton Boys' Dormitory. I was trying to figure out why someone would try to kill my parents. The fact that some one had tried to kill them seemed to prove my theory that they were more than just simple museum guards.

"Scott, Matt." Trinity came running up behind us.

"Trinity?" I looked at her with surprise. "Why aren't you home? It's late." Trinity attended school at the Academy, but lived with her grandmother and her dad in the faculty housing across campus. Her mom had left them when Trinity was small, but her grandma was very strict about her curfew.

"Dad had to meet with Superintendent Hinkly about getting some new equipment, so I stayed with him," she explained. "You will never guess what happened."

Matt and I looked at each other worriedly.

"After today, nothing would shock me," I commented dryly.

"Winston was here this afternoon to transfer to the Academy." She glanced back as if he might be watching us even now. "He's staying in the room right next to yours."

# Chapter

"Winston? The punk from the game?" I groaned in dismay. More bad news to finish off a terrible day. "Are you sure?"

"Sorry, I saw him myself," Trinity affirmed sympathetically. "I thought you guys might want a little warning."

"Yeah, thanks," I said grimly. Not that it could do much good if he was on the same floor as us. There'd be no getting away from him. "We'll see you in the morning."

"Right. And good luck with Winston." Trinity smiled at me as she turned to go. "Oh, yeah, I forgot. Since you guys don't believe in luck, maybe your God will make him go away for you."

"Maybe if we pray hard enough, He will," Matt grumbled as we entered the dorm. "Now we have to deal with that spoiled brat every day. Just what we need."

"Not only that, but he'll be in our unit, too," I reminded him. Each floor of both the girls' and boys' dormitories made up a different unit. A senior was appointed unit commander and was responsible for making sure that all the rules were obeyed within his or her unit. Students were required to march with their unit in morning and evening formations and to participate with their unit for any intramural competitions. If Winston was on our floor, he was now part of our team.

"Maybe if we leave him alone, he won't bother us," I said, not even really convincing myself.

"Sure," Matt answered dryly. "Maybe he'll be the picture of kindness, too."

"It *is* a bit too much to expect." I smiled weakly as we climbed the carpeted stairs to the second floor. "The important thing is that we don't let him get to us."

"I'll try," Matt promised, looking at me seriously. "You know that."

I looked down the hall warily, in no mood to deal with Winston tonight. "I don't see him."

"Quick," Matt whispered. "Duck into our room before he can see us."

# A Tragic Introduction

We dashed to our room just across from the stairs and closed the door behind us. I glanced around our sparsely furnished room as if I thought Winston were going to pop out of one of the two bunks against the back wall or one of the desks or dressers pushed against each of the side walls. I stopped myself just short of throwing open one of the mirrored closets on either side of the door. This day was really getting to me.

"At least we don't have to deal with him until morning," Matt said, sitting down on the side of his bunk. He stripped his uniform jacket off and tossed it on the floor.

"I hope dealing with Winston doesn't interfere with our investigation," I commented as I changed my clothes. I carefully removed all the pins and insignias from my blue uniform shirt and tossed it into my laundry hamper. I hung my jacket on the back of my desk chair to keep it from becoming wrinkled. I hated to iron, but wrinkles could be serious trouble during morning inspections. "Maybe tomorrow we can find out more about that name we found."

"Yeah," Matt said halfheartedly as he kicked off his shoes. "I suppose we could."

My fingers brushed cool plastic as I checked my pants pockets. "I almost forgot. I found something else, too." I pulled the silver card out and showed it to Matt as I flipped my khakis into the hamper.

"Where did you find this?" Matt asked with surprise. He snatched the card out of my hand and looked it over carefully.

"On the ground outside the wreck." I answered, a bit taken aback by his reaction. "Why? Do you recognize it?"

"I've only seen one of these before." Matt answered, handing the card back to me. "I thought for a moment it might be Chris's, but his has a different number on it. I think its some sort of ID card. One of the agents investigating the crash probably dropped it."

"Maybe," I said doubtfully. Finding an ID card like Chris's at the scene of my parents' crash seemed to confirm my theory. Whatever agency Chris worked for, I was willing to bet that there weren't too many agents who went around dropping ID cards. "Maybe not. What if my parents really were working with Chris? It could be one of theirs."

"Scott," Matt said wearily, pulling back the covers on his tightly made bed and crawling in. "If your parents were real law enforcement agents, don't you think you would have known by now?"

"Probably not. You're not even exactly sure what Chris does," I snapped, tired of Matt constantly trying to discourage me.

He was silent for a moment, and I thought he'd decided to go to sleep. "Look, Scott." Matt rolled over and looked at me with pain in his eyes. "I remember how it felt when Mom died. I spent nearly a year waking up every morning expecting to find her making breakfast like she always did, expecting to find out that, somehow, everyone had been wrong. And every morning for nearly

# A Tragic Introduction

a year, I relived her death when I realized she wasn't there."

"What happened after a year?" I asked gently. Matt didn't usually talk about his Mom. She'd died when he was little and his family had been stationed overseas, but he'd never told me any more than that. I hadn't stopped to consider that my tragedy was causing him to relive his.

"I accepted the fact that she was dead." He grunted and rolled away from me again. His next words were nearly inaudible. "Maybe it'll be easier if you just accept it now."

I sat on the edge of my bed tracing the raised numbers on the card with my thumb. Matt's words had hit a nerve. I didn't want to spend my life in denial, but was it denial to want proof? Was it denial not to give up when I felt in my heart that they weren't dead? I had to be sure, or I would be plagued the rest of my life not by denial, but by the feeling that I never really knew what happened to my parents. Or worse, that I could have done something to find them.

"What's Chris's number?" I asked with renewed determination in my voice.

"What?" Matt sounded surprised by my question.

"His cell phone number. What is it?"

"You're not going to call him, now?" Matt rolled back over and stared at me. "It's late!"

"Come on, you know Chris doesn't get to bed before midnight anyway. Please, just give me the number."

Matt gave in, and I punched in the numbers on the phone sitting on the table between us as quickly as I could. I was right; Chris was still up. I told him quickly what I'd found.

"What was the number on the card?" Chris asked.

"Six-three-one-one," I read.

"Six-three-one-one," Chris repeated. His voice sounded strangely grim. "Are you sure?"

I double checked the number on the card, even though I'd memorized it by now. "Yes, why?"

"I'll come for it first thing in the morning," Chris said sharply. "Don't lose it and don't show it to anyone else."

"Whose is…" It was too late, Chris had already hung up.

"What was that all about?" Matt asked as I hung up the phone.

"I don't know." I answered, looking thoughtfully at the phone. "He's coming over for the card first thing in the morning. He acted like it was really important."

After we exchanged "good nights," I switched the light off and lay down to sleep. Sleep couldn't come. I played over and over in my mind the many times my parents came home late, always with an excuse. Excuses I had never questioned, until now. Like the fact that they wouldn't let me stay home alone. Or the time Dad had an

# A Tragic Introduction

"accident" and Mom wouldn't let me leave the house for three weeks. That was when they'd sent me to the Academy.

I had always thought they were just being paranoid, but what if they really feared for my life? I never had understood exactly why they'd sent me to a military school, instead of any other boarding school if they just didn't want me home alone. If they were more than just regular security guards, maybe they had thought I would be safer at the Academy.

It also made me wonder even more what Chris's job was. If the danger they faced came from work, did he face that kind of danger, too? Matt was already snoring, so I couldn't pump him for more details about Chris's work. Not that I was even sure he could give me any more details. He hadn't seemed all that curious about what his brother did. To be honest, until today I hadn't been all that curious about my parents either.

*Lord, help me to figure out what's going on.* It was going to be a long night.

I awoke at 0600, dragged myself out of bed, showered, and pull my clothes on. As I buttoned the gold buttons on my blue jacket, I glanced at myself in the mirrored closet door. I adjusted my belt to make sure my gig-line - the line made by my jacket buttons, belt buckle, and pants zipper - was straight. I was in a hurry, but I didn't want to get demerits for being out of uniform. A wrinkle in my sharply pressed khaki pants or a scuff in my highly polished black shoes could be enough to get me three demerits.

# Jessica C. Joiner

Grabbing the silver card from off the nightstand, I looked at it carefully. *I wonder if it could be my Dad's.* I scowled as I stuffed it into my back pocket. *I wonder if Chris will actually tell me the truth, not just play games with me.*

I made my bed and prepared my room for inspections mechanically. The time it took to make everything suitable for morning inspections made me impatient, but I forced myself to take the time to clean my room right. If an Academy student received more than one demerit in any given week, he could be restricted to the campus over the weekend.

*I can't risk that.* I sighed as I smoothed a wrinkle out of my bed sheets. *I can't afford to lose one day that I might be able to use to find my parents.*

Matt finished long before me and went down for breakfast. His side of the room was always messier than mine, but somehow he always finished faster than I did. I wasn't in the mood for breakfast, but I made my way slowly across the campus to the student commons anyway. My head ached, and I was tired from my sleepless night. The buzz of conversation as I entered the cafeteria made my head hurt more.

Finding an empty table, I sat down to a bowl of cereal, picked at it moodily, and finally went down with the other students to the parade grounds for morning formation. My mind miles away, I went through the routine like a robot, focused instead on my parents and what I was going to do to get them back.

"Cadet McCully!" Sergeant Mason barked.

# A Tragic Introduction

"Sir, yes, sir!" I snapped to attention and saluted. My eyes went wide with both fear and confusion at being called out.

"Didn't you hear me?"

"No, sir." I gulped. Actually, I hadn't heard a word he had said all morning.

"You and Cadet Marshall have a visitor in the Superintendent's office. Now march!"

I marched double time until I was out of sight and then ran as fast as I could to the Superintendent's office. Matt arrived shortly afterwards, panting from his attempt to keep up with me.

"Hello, Scott, Matt," Chris greeted us wearily. He was leaning back in Superintendent Hinkly's chair. His tired eyes glanced at the chairs in front of him, indicating that Matt and I were to take a seat. He looked like he'd slept less than I had.

"Hey, Chris." I pulled the card out of my back pocket. "This is the card I found."

"Where did you find it?" Chris asked. He took the card from my hand and pocketed it without even glancing at it.

I hesitated before answering. "At the crash site, under a fallen tree limb."

"I'm not even going to ask what you were doing at the crash site," Chris said, apparently too tired to reprimand me. "I think I can guess."

"What's so important about that card?" I steered the conversation back on track, and me away from trouble.

"It's kind of like a badge," Chris explained. The leather chair creaked as he leaned back. He looked at Matt and me carefully, as if trying to make a decision. He finally sighed. "It's not really what it is that's important, but who it belonged to."

"Someone important?" I asked, leaning forward expectantly.

"You could say that." Chris frowned as if second-guessing his choice to talk. "It belonged to Agent Eric McCully. It probably fell to the ground when our men removed his belongings from the plane."

"So Scott's dad did work with you?" Matt turned to me apologetically. "You were right!"

"His dad and mom, actually," Chris answered, watching my reaction carefully "They were two of our top agents."

"So you work for Global Security Services as well?" I asked slowly, my eyes challenging him to lie to me.

He pulled a business card out of his wallet and laid it on the table in front of us. It read, "Global Security Services, Agent Christopher Marshall."

So he did work with my parents. I'd known him for three years and no one had felt it necessary to mention that fact?

# A Tragic Introduction

"What, exactly, is Global Security Services?" I pushed the words through my clenched teeth. "And don't even think to tell me it's a security firm."

Chris stood abruptly from the chair, crossed to the door, and locked it. I glanced over at Matt and met his raised eyebrow. Perhaps now we were going to get some answers.

"Global Security Services *is* a security firm." Chris sat back in the chair, rested his elbows on the desk and templed his fingers. "It is also one of many covers for SATURN." He laid a second card beside the first, a near duplicate of the one I'd found by the wreck.

"And that is?" I tried to keep the exasperation from my voice, but failed. Could he *be* any more vague?

"Secret Agent Training University and Reconnaissance Network." Matt breathed in awe. "I thought it was a military myth."

"A spy agency?" I said doubtfully. "You're telling me that you and my parents are spies?"

"Secret agents," Chris corrected, inclining his head. "Your parents headed up the most elite team in the organization."

I didn't feel as elated by the revelation as I had thought I would. Instead, I felt confused and hurt that my parents would hide such a large part of their lives from me. *They're spies. It's part of their jobs.* As if that made their double lives all right. I wasn't going to allow my feelings about their secrets to get to me. I could deal with that after I found them.

"I was beginning to suspect that they worked with you," I admitted, my thoughts returning to the day before. "You were too upset yesterday when you told me about their crash."

Chris drew a deep breath. "Eric and Marisa – your parents – were my mentors. More than that, they were my friends." His Adam's apple bobbed and he dropped his clenched fists to the desk. "Someone suspected they worked for SATURN." A hint of anger threaded his voice. "I'm doing everything I can to find out who."

"If Matt and I think of anything else that might help, we'll let you know," I promised smoothly.

"Absolutely not. Under no circumstances are you to get involved in this." Chris's expression hardened as he stood to leave. "I know you want to help, but the people who did this are not like your average school bullies. They mean business. We've got this under control; just leave it to the professionals. Okay?"

Matt and I were silent. I didn't want to do or say anything that might make Chris angry, but there was no way I was making that promise, not when I was only now beginning to find out who my parents really were.

Our silence didn't go unnoticed. Narrowing his eyes, Chris pressed his hands on the desk and leaned toward us. His brown eyes held a haunted look. "I *will* find out what happened to them, but I couldn't stand it if either of you got hurt. For your own good, stay out of the way."

# Chapter

I met Chris's gaze with a challenge of my own.
They were my parents. I deserved to know the truth.

The corner of Chris's mouth twitched and he
raised an eyebrow. He stepped back and shook his head,
looking at me as if seeing me for the first time.

"I'll keep you in the loop, Scott." He offered his
hand and a tight smile. "Just try not to make trouble."

Wondering at his change in attitude, I took his
hand and shook it hesitantly.

"What was that about?" Matt asked as Chris left
us alone in the office.

# Jessica C. Joiner

"He's your brother." I shrugged and stuck my hands into my pockets as we got up to leave. My fingers brushed the slip of paper I had found at the crash.

"I forgot to give this to Chris." I groaned as pulled out the crumpled slip of paper in my hand and looked at it in dismay.

"We could try his cell phone number." Matt paused with his hand on the doorknob.

"I've got a better idea," I said slowly, "Let's try this number and see who this Hayes person is."

"Chris said…" Matt began reluctantly.

"I know what Chris said." I frowned. I was more interested in what Chris hadn't said than in what he had said. There were still too many unanswered questions. "But if we leave it to the 'professionals,' they'll only tell us what they think we need to know. Chris only told me that my parents worked with him because we found that card ourselves. I need to know everything. They're my parents!"

Ignoring Matt's look of disapproval, I used the phone on Superintendent Hinkly's desk to dial the number on the slip of paper rather than Chris's. After the tenth ring, I lowered the phone from my ear to hang up in frustration and try again later.

"Yeah?" gruff voice answered.

"Did you know an Eric McCully?" I jerked the phone back to my ear and winced. This phone number was my only lead, and I wanted to get to the point, but that just sounded desperate.

# A Tragic Introduction

"Who wants to know?"

"This is his son, Scott," I answered. "His plane went down a couple of days ago. We found your name and number in the wreck."

"I ain't talking to anyone," Hayes growled, "and I didn't have anything to do with the crash!"

"I'm not saying you did," I said quickly. *Please don't let him hang up!* "It's just… You're my only lead. I thought you might know something."

"Look, kid, your parents were nice," Hayes said, his voice softening a little, "but I don't have anything to say to you."

"Can you at least tell me what information you had for them?" I gave up trying not to sound desperate, even considered begging. If this didn't work, I was left with waiting on Chris to toss me whatever crumbs of redacted info his agency decided he could share.

"Why should I?"

"Maybe you did have something to do with the crash after all." I changed my approach. In the movies, most secret contacts weren't quite friendly with the law. I edged my voice with a sharp threat. "Perhaps I ought to just give your name to the police…"

"No, don't do that." Hayes sighed heavily. "I have no idea what a kid would do with my information, but that's your business. Meet me at Catonsville Community Park at midnight."

"Midnight?" I bit my lip and glanced at Matt's irritated expression. He shook his head violently and mouthed something that looked like, "Are you insane?".

That was two hours after curfew.

"The guys who knocked off your parents might be watching me," Hayes pointed out. "Midnight."

"We'll be there," I promised and hung up.

"Midnight!" Matt exclaimed, scowling at me. "What's wrong with you? How are we going to get out after curfew?"

"Over the fence," I said grimly. "Catonsville Community Park is close enough to walk."

"We could get in real trouble for this." Matt lowered his voice and leaned forward against the back of a chair. "We're not talking about push-ups any more. If we get caught, we'll be expelled!"

"I know." I had never broken academy rules before – at least not intentionally - but I *had* to find out about my parents. Their lives could be at stake, and I was willing to take the consequences of breaking curfew to save them. I crossed the office and opened the door. "Hayes is my only lead, and I have to follow it up. You don't have to come along."

"I still think we ought to let Chris take care of this," Matt whispered as we entered the crowded hall on our way to class. We had already missed the rest of morning formation, but if we hurried, we would be in time for our first period class.

# A Tragic Introduction

"Don't you see?" I stopped walking and turned to face Matt. I had to make him understand how important following up on this lead was to me. "I have to find out what happened to them. I don't even know for sure if my parents are really dead. Wouldn't you feel the same way if someone just came and told you Chris had disappeared?"

A pained look crossed Matt's face and he looked away. "Yeah." He ran his hand through his short brown hair. "But I'm not going to let you go by yourself. I'm sticking with you, no matter what happens or however long it takes."

I clapped him on the back and gave him a lopsided grin. "I really appreciate that." Not that I expected any different.

"Yeah, well." Matt chuckled weakly. "I'd appreciated it if you'd at least *try* to keep us out of trouble."

"We'll be in huge trouble if we don't get to Physics." I hustled into the classroom behind another pair of students. "I'm having enough trouble in that class without showing up late to it."

We slipped behind our desks just as Professor Davidson was beginning roll call.

I really did try to pay attention as Professor Davidson droned on about electrons, protons, and other equally confusing topics. I was already well on my way to failing the class if I couldn't get my grades up, but the events of the last couple of days filled my thoughts and blocked out the professor's monotonous lecture.

# Jessica C. Joiner

*Dear Lord, please allow this meeting with Hayes to give me some answers about my parents. I really...*

"Cadet McCully." Professor Davidson's impatient voice interrupted my prayer.

I snapped to attention beside my desk while trying to recall some part of the lecture. I couldn't remember a word.

"Well, Cadet McCully." Professor Davidson tapped his pointer against his palm as he frowned at me. "Do you have an answer?"

"Could you repeat the question, sir?" I felt my face grow hot as the other students snickered.

"Would it perhaps help if I repeated the entire lecture up to this point?" Professor Davidson asked dryly. "You can hardly expect your grades to rise if you insist on daydreaming in class. You may be seated, Cadet McCully."

I caught a sympathetic glance from Matt as I sat back down. Professor Davidson's remark stung; I wasn't normally so easily distracted. Forcing aside my swirling thoughts, I kept my eyes focused on Professor Davidson as he called on another student. I wasn't about to be accused of daydreaming again.

"Cadet Daytona," Professor Davidson addressed a dark-haired boy seated in the front row.

I groaned inwardly as Winston proudly stood to attention and answered the question easily. "Electrons have the negative charge, sir. Protons are positive."

# A Tragic Introduction

"Very good, Cadet Daytona." Professor Davidson smiled at him as he sat back down. "Perhaps after classes are over, you could fill Cadet McCully in on what he missed."

"Certainly, Professor Davidson," Winston answered sweetly, his perfect posture and neatly folded hands adding to the illusion of a perfect student. "If he'll let me."

"Hm." Professor Davidson grunted and directed his next comment at me. "He'd better let someone help him if he expects to pass."

*Great!* I slid down in my chair. *As if I need to be tutored by* him *in addition to everything else that has happened.*

After we were dismissed, I gathered my books and left quickly to avoid having Winston offer his "help." Merging into the hallway, I tried to make my way unnoticed to my next class.

"Come on, Scott, wait up!" I turned to see Matt and Trinity coming down the hall. I slowed to allow them to catch up.

"You okay?" Matt scanned my face with concern.

"I guess so." I yanked open my locker and slammed my physics book inside. "Professor Davidson was right. I shouldn't have allowed myself to be distracted in class, not with my grades the way they are."

"What happened?" Trinity fell in step beside me as we continued down the hall. "You don't usually slack off in class."

## Jessica C. Joiner

Glancing at Matt on my other side, I sighed and pretended to reorganize my locker. I couldn't keep putting her off, but knowing that didn't make finding the words any easier. I blew out a long breath and looked up at her. "My parents' plane went down outside of town yesterday."

"Oh, Scott!" Her eyes grew wide. "I'm so sorry."

Clenching my jaw tightly, I looked back into my locker as a wave of emotion hit me. Talking to Matt about their deaths was entirely different than talking to Trinity. I wanted to explain everything to her, but I couldn't. I couldn't really even explain it to myself yet.

"What's the deal with Winston?" Matt changed the subject. "He's suddenly acting super nice."

"He's trying to get in good with the teachers." Trinity scowled and twisted her locket between her fingers in frustration. "Before Professor Davidson came to class, Winston was bragging that he could make the teachers love him and get away with murder."

"Well, he's certainly got Professor Davidson fooled." I frowned, remembering the look Professor Davidson had given me.

"He'll have a long road to fool the students, though." Trinity paused when we came to an intersection in the hall, dropped her locket, and waved. "Anyway, I've got to get to my next class. I'll see you guys later."

As Trinity turned to head toward her classroom, Matt and I continued slowly toward ours. We had only

## A Tragic Introduction

five minutes between each class, but I was in no mood to hurry.

"At least Winston doesn't have every class with us." Matt commented. "I saw him turn down that hall just before Trinity."

"Leave him alone, you bully!" A muffled voice came from the other hall.

"That sounded like Trinity!" I grabbed Matt's arm and turned back to the intersection.

"Since when is this any of your business?" A high-pitched whine followed from the same direction.

"And that sounded like Winston!" Matt returned hotly, barreling down the other hallway. "Come on!"

# Chapter

We followed Trinity's voice to an empty classroom on our left. She stood inside, hands on her hips, facing Winston, who was holding a smaller student against the chalkboard. How he had actually found a student smaller than him was beyond me.

"Cadet Miller was just offering to help me do my homework." Winston smiled at Trinity wickedly.

"I'll bet he was." Trinity's blue eyes flashed and her angry face was about as red as her hair. "It looks like you're doing more forcing than he's offering. Let go of him!"

# Jessica C. Joiner

I scanned the hall to see if I could get the attention of a teacher. The hall was loud as students rifled through their lockers preparing for their next class period, but most of the teachers were already in their classrooms.

"I wasn't hurting him," Winston said, releasing his grip before turning to Trinity. As soon as Winston's back was turned, the frightened student slipped between Matt and me and disappeared into the crowded hall. "We were just negotiating a business proposition. This wasn't any of your concern."

"The real truth is you're just a bully." Trinity shot back.

"I'm not the bully around here!" Winston shouted, taking a step toward Trinity. "You are. You think that because your dad's a teacher, you can get away with picking on the new kid."

I tried to catch Trinity's eye as I drew my hand across my throat in a signal to let it go. She didn't even seem to see me, and I didn't dare leave Matt alone with Winston while I went to track down a teacher

"I'm not picking on you," Trinity choked out, her clenched fists dropping to her sides. "You were picking on Cadet Miller."

Behind me, Matt behind me snorted like a bull about to charge. If I didn't do something fast I would have a full-fledged brawl on my hands.

"Cadet Miller?" Winston stepped forward and got in her face, even though Trinity was still slightly taller than he was. He seemed to be trying to make up for his

# A Tragic Introduction

shortness with meanness. "I already told you we had a business agreement."

"Back off, Winston." I struggled to control my own anger as I stepped next to Trinity. I kept my voice low and threatening and hoped Winston would get the point. "Don't you have anything better to do than to pick on a girl?"

"She started it," Winston whimpered. He took a step back and glared up at me as Matt stepped in to back me up.

"Whatever," I snapped. "Matt and I saw the whole thing. Get lost."

Winston seethed for a moment. Then he looked at me with a nasty glint in his eyes and said, "I heard what happened to your parents, Cadet McCully. You should be glad. Dead parents can't chew you out for failing school."

The room grew very quiet.

*Dear, Lord!* I closed my eyes and stood stiffly, clenching and unclenching my fists. *Help me to control my temper. Help me not to give in to his goading!*

"You horrible little…" Trinity gasped beside me.

Taking a deep breath to force myself to calm down, I opened my eyes and looked at Winston. He was chuckling to himself as if he had just told an amusing joke. I tightened my fist and fought the urge to wipe his smug grin right off his face.

"You think that's funny?" Matt took a step toward Winston with his fist cocked. "I'll show you something I think is really funny, you monster!"

# Jessica C. Joiner

"Don't, Matt," I whispered, putting my arm out to hold my friend back. In spite of Winston's nastiness, I was aware that our Christian testimony in front of Trinity was at stake here. I wasn't going to blow it.

"But, Scott." Matt waved his fist at Winston, who only looked at him with defiance, as if daring Matt to hit him. "He…"

"That's just what he wants – a reaction," I continued in the same even tone, "I'm not going to lower myself to his level. Let's just go to class. Come on, Trinity."

Taking Matt by his still upraised arm, I turned to lead my friends back out to the hall just as the bell rang. We were going to be late for class, but at least we had avoided a fight. For now.

"Sure, walk away, McCully," Winston called after us. "I knew you were a sissy!"

"Keep walking," I advised through clenched teeth. I tugged at Matt's arm, but there was no way I could hold him back if he allowed Winston to get to him. "Remember your testimony and just ignore him."

"How can you stand to be seen in public with such a wimp, Cadet Marshall?" Winston changed his target to the one who seemed to be reacting. "I'd be embarrassed to admit he was my friend!"

"That's enough!" Matt roared, tearing his arm from my grasp and rushing back toward Winston.

Trinity gasped as Winston dodged Matt's punch and ducked behind the teacher's desk.

# A Tragic Introduction

"You tried to hit me!" Winston shrieked. "You took a swing at me. I never hurt anyone."

"Oh, great," I muttered, stepping between the howling Winston and the now embarrassed Matt. "Knock it off, Winston, you're not hurt."

"He tried though. If I hadn't ducked, he'd have hit me!" Winston continued to holler. His screams would finally bring the teacher I'd failed to find earlier.

"I'm going to Superintendent Hinkly," Winston threatened Matt, his voice closer to normal volume as he stood from behind the desk and jabbed his finger at Matt. "You're the real bully, trying to hurt a smaller student."

"You started it. Besides, I didn't even touch you," Matt protested and then appealed to me. "You can vouch for me, can't you?"

"Explain that to Superintendent Hinkly," Winston sneered. "You can't keep me from telling him what happened!"

"Not even going to try." I shrugged. I was going to call his bluff. He wouldn't dare go to Superintendent Hinkly.

"You're not?" Winston actually looked disappointed.

"You're not?" Trinity repeated, stepping away from the classroom door toward us.

"But, Scott," Matt said, looking at me with confusion. "Superintendent Hinkly will…"

"Superintendent Hinkly will want to hear both sides of the story." I cut in and turned to look Winston in the eye. "If you want Superintendent Hinkly to hear about your behavior toward Cadet Miller, go right ahead."

Winston looked at me. His mouth worked frantically, but no sound came out, and his face flamed to a deep red.

"I'll get you guys later," he finally managed to snarl as he shoved past us into the hall.

"Thanks, Scott," Matt said, letting out a relieved sigh.

"No problem." I smiled at my friend. "Just try not to let his taunting make you lose your cool. He's just trying to make trouble."

"I want to thank you, too." Trinity stepped forward and smiled warmly at me. "I'm glad you stood up for me."

"It was nothing," I said, rubbing the back of my neck in embarrassment. My face grew warm in spite of myself. "Just helping out a friend, that's all."

"Man," Matt groaned as he glanced down the empty hallway. "That bully made us late to class."

Parting quickly, we hurried to our separate classes. Perhaps if we were lucky we could avoid any further confrontations – at least for the rest of the day.

As soon as dinner was over, Matt and I hurried to our room to prepare for the night's activities. Many of the students left for home as soon as the last bell rang on Fridays, so I hoped that it would be easy to escape the nearly empty campus.

# A Tragic Introduction

After lights out, Matt and I stepped out of our room into the carpeted hall. Our unit commander had already checked on everyone to make sure that each cadet was in bed, so the hall was empty, but even the slightest noise could bring a curious cadet out to investigate.

We slipped down the stairs and glanced carefully out the front doors before opening them. The doors could always be opened from the inside, in case of an emergency, but were diligently locked at curfew. I jammed a wad of paper tightly into the latch to keep it from locking us out. Not even students could get in after lights out. My heart pounded nervously as we quietly slipped out of the building.

We ducked into the bushes on the side closest to the fence. I peered through the branches, timing carefully how long it took for the student watchman to make his rounds. Once I was sure the coast was clear, I nodded to Matt, and we dashed across the lawn to the fence and scrambled over. JJMA wasn't really built with security in mind, and the fence was almost more of a warning. We quickly hid in the trees on the other side of the fence as the watchman made his way back.

Once soon as he was gone again, we continued toward the park. In less than fifteen minutes, we were standing underneath a lamppost at Catonsville Community Park. The ease of our escape made me feel elated – and nervous. If anyone noticed that we were gone, getting back in would be nearly impossible, at least not without getting expelled.

"I guess we won't have any trouble identifying Hayes," I commented as I looked around the empty park. "No one else is out here at this time of night."

Matt looked around at the dark outlines of trees and benches and shifted his weight. "I'll be glad when we get back to the Academy. It's just a little creepy out here at night."

I nodded my agreement. "We've already come this far; we can't turn back now."

It was past midnight and I was beginning to wonder if Hayes had changed his mind when a shadowy figure walked toward us and stopped just outside the light of the lamppost.

"Which of you is the McCullys' kid?" the figure asked.

"I am." My heart raced as I recognized the voice as the one I had heard on the phone. I took a step closer to the shadow. "Are you Hayes?"

"Yes, listen carefully. I'll tell you all I know. Then I'll leave, and you never saw me. Understand?"

"Yes."

"Your parents were looking for the Snake. Wanted to keep him from stealing a weapon."

"What kind of weapon?" Matt interrupted roughly.

"Supposedly it sends out some sort of radiation that causes electrical devices to short out," Hayes answered. "Anyway, I was going to be in on the job and

## A Tragic Introduction

was supposed to tell them when the heist was going down, but they never showed up."

"Who's the Snake?" It wasn't too much of a stretch to imagine that the same person who wanted the weapon had caused the crash to keep my parents from getting in the way.

Hayes was silent for a moment. I wasn't sure if he was debating whether to give that important a piece of information to a pair of teenagers, or if even he had no idea.

"Hey, you guys!" a whiny voice called from the darkness.

Hayes jumped, muttered something about a trap, and disappeared into the shadows.

"Wait!" I shouted into the darkness, before whirling in anger toward the voice that had interrupted us just as I was about get a lead on my parents.

"If that's who I think it is," Matt seethed. "I'm going to kill him!"

Winston stepped into the light of the lamppost.

"What are you doing here?" I demanded, not even bothering to hide my irritation..

"I overheard you two talking about your little meeting earlier today." Winston grinned. "You think you're great detectives, but you never even noticed that I was following you!"

"We have a perfectly good reason for being out here tonight," I said evenly. Blowing up at Winston would not bring Hayes back, no matter how tempting it was choke the little weasel right now.

"That'll come in handy when you try to explain to Superintendent Hinkly," Winston answered. The shadows from the street lamp emphasized the evil grin that spread across his face. "Unless…"

"Unless, what?" I said tightly, forcing myself to sound calm.

"Unless you let me help," Winston said. "I can play detective just as well as you."

"No," Matt said sharply. "I'd rather take my chances with Superintendent Hinkly."

"You two can't hog all the fun!" Winston whined. "It's not fair!"

"This isn't a game, Winston," I said through clenched teeth, rage boiling inside me. The events of the past two days were pushing me to a breaking point. "We don't need your help."

"You're going to need someone's help," Winston said vindictively, "after I turn you in to Superintendent Hinkly."

# Chapter

Sitting in the waiting room to the superintendent's office at one in the morning has to be one of the most nerve-wracking things I've ever done. Especially sitting there thinking that you're probably going to be expelled and knowing that you deserved it.

I groaned and dropped my head into my hands. To top it off, I was no closer to finding anything out about my parents. The whole trip had been a waste, and I'd sabotaged my senior year for nothing.

"Where is he?" Matt whispered. His leg bounced relentlessly, jiggling the chair beside me. "We've been here for more than an hour."

Superintendent Hinkly had given us a disapproving glare, locked us into the waiting room, and left. I assumed he was getting the deans to discuss our punishment; a punishment not likely to be merciful at one in the morning.

Matt bounced his leg faster until my own chair started shaking. "We're going to be expelled," he moaned. "I know it!"

"We both have good records; they have no reason not to be lenient." I tried to sound more confident than I felt. "You're overreacting."

"That's easy for you to say," Matt said sharply, turning quickly to face me. "Your parents don't expect you to be the next General Patton! My dad will never forgive me if I get kicked out of the Academy."

"I'm just worried about *finding* my parents." I stared vacantly out the window behind the empty receptionist's desk. "If Superintendent Hinkly expels us, I'll probably be sent to my grandparents' ranch in Texas. How will I find the truth about my parents then? I'm not thinking the distance is going to make your brother more generous with his information."

"You're right." Matt slouched in his chair and covered his face with his hands. "I'm sorry I lost my temper. I guess…" He blew out a long breath. "We really messed up this time, didn't we?"

# A Tragic Introduction

"Yeah, I guess we did." *God, forgive me.* I knew better. In all that had happened after my parents' plane went down, I'd never stopped to think about what was the *right* thing to do. "We need to pray, Matt. If we'd done that to begin with, we might not be in this mess."

"Yeah, I guess we blew it in more than one way," Matt agreed, shame tinting his ears.

"Lord Jesus, please forgive us for breaking the school rules and going out after curfew," I began. "Please allow Superintendent Hinkly to have mercy on us. Help us to be a better example of our faith to those around us. Amen."

"Amen," Matt echoed, looking up at me. "Are we going to tell them everything?"

"Yes… I don't know." I rubbed my temples to ward off the beginnings of a throbbing headache. "Our part, at least. I don't even know what to make about my parents' role in all this. If we apologize for sneaking out, maybe he'll only put us on probation."

A key clicked in the lock and the door to hall opened with a creak. My stomach twisted as Matt and I snapped to attention and saluted weakly.

It wasn't Superintendent Hinkly at the door, or the deans. The man at the door wasn't anyone I recognized at all. He was tall, with black hair going gray at the temples and a build that suggested he'd once been an athlete. An expensive, tailored suit nearly hid the bulge of a concealed weapon at his side. His lips were pressed in a grim line and his alert, dark eyes seemed to be weighing our judgment already. His manner shouted authority, and fear rippled up my spine as I wondered if this was the man who would decide our fate.

I pulled my back straighter and held my salute as the man entered and crossed to us. He stopped in front of me and frowned.

"Cadet Scott Eric McCully, twelfth grade," he spoke as if reading a report. "AB honor role, but struggles in science. Star quarterback and decent pitcher. Attends church regularly; no past history of trouble."

My breath caught in my chest. How did this complete stranger know so much about me? Had Superintendent Hinkly told him?

"Cadet Matthew David Marshall, also a senior." He stepped over to Matt and continued, "B average grades that slip during football season. Enjoys video games and war movies. Deeply religious, but struggles with a quick temper."

"Sir, yes, sir." Matt's face was white and his eyes wide, but he still stood frozen at attention.

"You look just like your brother." The man nodded as if satisfied. "At ease."

I let out a slow breath and relaxed, a little.

"You know my brother, sir?" Matt asked warily.

"I know everything there is about you both." The man darted a meaningful glance at me. "Perhaps more than you know about yourselves."

"You work with Chris." I clenched my hands into fists to keep them from shaking. If Superintendent Hinkly

# A Tragic Introduction

had called in SATURN, we were in even more trouble than I thought.

"You're half right," Chris replied from where he leaned against the doorway with his arms crossed. He was dressed more casually than before, wearing a pair of jeans and a dark blue tee shirt that did little to hide a handgun stuffed into his waistband. I hadn't even noticed him come in. "Scott, Matt, I'd like to introduce you to Mr. Alan Jackson, my boss."

We saluted again, but I couldn't shake the feeling that this was just getting worse.

"When Superintendent Hinkly called and told me that you two had been caught sneaking out after curfew, I reached the same conclusion he did." Chris stood beside his boss and gave us a disappointed frown. "I told you two to leave the investigation to me. Do you have any idea how stupid this was? How incredibly dangerous?"

"Perhaps we should take this to the superintendent's office, Agent Marshall," Mr. Jackson suggested, his deep voice a warning.

Chris clenched his jaw, gave a sharp nod, and motioned for us to follow Mr. Jackson into the office.

"Be seated, boys." Mr. Jackson sat in Superintendent Hinkly's chair and waved his hand to the chairs facing the desk. "Tell me about tonight."

I bit my lip as we sat and Chris closed the door behind us then perched on the corner of the desk. At this point, our only hope was telling them everything and hoping they didn't arrest us.

# Jessica C. Joiner

"Sir, Matt and I found a slip of paper at the crash site that mentioned a man my parents were supposed to meet – a Hayes." I glanced at Chris and tried to keep the bitterness out of my voice, "Since Chris hadn't been very… generous… with his information, I decided to investigate myself."

"The secrets are there for your protection, Scott," Chris said with exasperation in his voice. "You met an informant, at midnight, without backup. Not even a trained agent does that. Not any of the smart ones at least."

"Okay, I get it, it was dumb," I snapped, then remembered that I was already in enough trouble and began again more carefully, "It was wrong and stupid. And I'm sorry." I gave Mr. Jackson a challenging look. "But what am I supposed to do? Chris isn't telling me everything. I'm not even sure my parents are actually dead." My words rushed over one another as I continued, "Chris didn't even tell me they worked with him until I found Dad's card. That leaves me to find out for myself, with or without SATURN's help."

The room was silent for a moment. Matt looked at me worriedly, as if hoping I knew what I was doing. I just hoped I wasn't digging us a deeper hole.

"I told you," Chris said finally, looking to Mr. Jackson. His mouth was still grim, but a hint of a smile lit his eyes.

"Indeed." Mr. Jackson sighed. He turned his critical gaze to Matt. "Cadet Marshall, you've been

## A Tragic Introduction

noticeably silent. Can I trust you to keep out of the way, or do you always do what Cadet McCully does?"

"Scott's my best friend, sir. I'm behind him as long as he's involved," Matt answered. His voice was firm, but his eyes showed he didn't entirely agree with my decision. "I won't abandon my friend."

Mr. Jackson rubbed the bridge of his nose while Chris snickered. "Agent Marshall warned me that Cadet McCully had too much of his father in him to stand by while we investigated." He tossed a sideways glance at Chris. "And Cadet Marshall is clearly too much like his brother to expect him to leave his friend's side."

A troubled look crossed Chris's face, and he glared down at his clenched fist.

"Agent Marshall had a suggestion to keep the two of you out of trouble." Mr. Jackson gave us one more sweeping look and nodded. "After tonight, I'm inclined to agree to his recommendation."

Keeping us out of trouble didn't exactly sound like helping find out what happened to my parents, but it was better than expulsion – or jail – so I decided to listen.

"Your parent's were assigned to protect an inventor named Isaac Kestler," Chris began. "He was perfecting a device that could revolutionize warfare: an EMP transmitter that would knock out any electronic device within a ten mile radius."

"Ten miles?" Matt leaned forward, gripping the arms of his chair. "That'd cover the whole city of Baltimore!"

"You mean that device could take out all the phones, computers, and appliances in the whole city?" I tried to imagine Baltimore in the dark, but the impact of losing everything that ran on electricity blew my mind.

"Worse than that." Mr. Jackson stood and clasped his hands behind his back. "Power grids are connected. A device like that could knock out utilities across the Eastern seaboard. It was critical that SATURN keep that invention out of the wrong hands." He tossed a sharp glance at Chris.

I noted his use of the word "was" and flashed a wide-eyed look to Chris.

Chris sat up straighter and a red tint colored his neck. "We doubled security on Kestler so your parents could meet with Hayes about an attack he was supposedly involved in. They were going to try to make your game while they were in town. They... never made it."

"Did you find their bodies?" I asked a bit too bluntly. "Not to be gross or anything, but I was at the wreck. There's no blood, no personal effects, nothing. How can you be sure they're dead?"

"We're quite sure." Mr. Jackson cut off any comment Chris was going to make with a wave of his hand. "We found an empty canister of Sarin gas in the wreckage. Even if they had survived the crash, even a small dose of that would have killed them. We'll find the bodies." He sounded confident, and like he'd had this conversation before.

Chris frowned, pulled the sunglasses from his collar, snapped them open, and put them on. Either

# A Tragic Introduction

rehearsing the story of my parents' deaths was upsetting him more than he wanted to let on, or he didn't agree with SATURN's conclusion any more than I did.

"Eric and Marisa's deaths strained our resources." Mr. Jackson shot Chris another hard look, one I now interpreted to be a warning, and went back to pacing. "With my agents divided between investigating the crash and protecting Dr. Kestler, we were unable to keep his lab from being attacked. Dr. Kestler was saved, but his invention was lost."

"So you're telling us someone has the ability to send half the US into the dark ages?" Matt's jaw tightened and the skeptical look he'd given me disappeared. "What can we do to help?"

"Dr. Kestler is the only one who can work his invention." Chris crossed his arms over his chest. "Unfortunately, after SATURN's failure to protect his invention, Kestler's not interested in accepting our help."

"That's where you boys come in." Mr. Jackson dropped back into his chair and folded his hands in front of him. "We've got his house watched twenty-four seven, but need someone on the inside. Someone to open conversation, maybe make sure no one contacts him to negotiate a trade."

"Maybe even plant a bug for us," Chris added.

"How exactly are we going to do that?" I asked skeptically. "It's not like he's just going to let a couple of teens into his house."

"Actually, he is." Chris smiled at us. "Dr. Kestler tutors high-schoolers in science, sort of his way to give back. I've already spoken to Superintendent Hinkly about finding a tutor for the two of you. He agreed wholeheartedly." Chris removed his glasses and gestured at me. "Apparently he's already aware you guys need the help."

"You mean, we won't be expelled?" Matt slouched back in his chair and blew out a long breath.

"Your superintendent agreed to place you on disciplinary probation, due to the rather difficult extenuating circumstances." Mr. Jackson stood, straightened his suit, and gave us a severe look. "As long as the two of you can stay out of trouble from now on. Consider this your warning."

# Chapter

That following Monday as soon as school was out, Matt and I left armed with our Physics text books, paper, pencils, and a half dozen tiny transmitters that looked like dimes.

Chris had recommended we just "lose" them in various places in the house. The idea of bugging the house made me a little nervous. And more than a little excited.

"If nothing else, maybe you'll actually be able to pass physics." Matt grinned at me from the passenger's seat of my car. Our narrow escape from expulsion and our new adventure seemed to have him in high spirits as well.

"Hey." I pretended to be offended. "You could use the help, too."

"At least, I'm not failing," Matt ribbed. "I may be close, but I'm not quite there yet."

"So science isn't my thing," I admitted with a shrug. "Can I help it if I find it boring?"

"And there are so many more interesting things in that classroom." Matt winked at me. "Like Trinity."

I punched Matt's leg. "Trinity's a good friend, that's all."

"A really, really good friend." His grin widened as he rubbed his leg.

"And that's all she can be as long as we don't see eye to eye about Christ." I stared at the road in front of me. Trinity couldn't seem to get past the fact that she was too a good person to need God in her life. I shook my head. "Besides, she'd get tired of me going to church all the time. We're better off just friends."

"I know." Matt nodded, still smiling. "It's still fun to tease you about her. If she ever does get saved, you'd better watch out. I think she likes you."

"I certainly hope she does." I paused to glare at Matt's amused look and added irritably, "Get saved soon, I mean."

Her lack of interest bothered me more than I wanted Matt to know, so I took a quick breath and

# A Tragic Introduction

changed the subject. "What do you think Dr. Kestler will be like?"

"Probably old, with crazy gray hair." Matt formed his hands into "O's" and held them up to his eyes. "And huge glasses, like a mad scientist..."

He broke off abruptly as we neared the address Superintendent Hinkly had given us. "Nice."

I looked at what he was staring at. A shiny, rebuilt Ford Model T was sitting in the driveway of an ivy covered Victorian era house. It looked right at home, and Matt looked like he was going to start drooling.

"Now who's distracted?" I laughed as I turned my car into gravel driveway and parked behind the Model T. The contrast between Dr. Kestler's pristine classic and my junker was actually funny. "Keep in mind what we're here for – tutoring and spying." A thought hit me. "Do you think he'll suspect us?"

"Teens? Working for SATURN?" Matt tore his eyes from the shiny, black car and snorted. "He'd have to be really paranoid."

"Still." I turned the ignition off and opened my door. "We'd better be careful; we don't want to blow our only chance to help."

The gravel crunched under our feet as Matt and I walked up the drive to the house. We turned up the brick walk leading to Dr. Kestler's Victorian home. It was a large, two-story house that looked as if the ivy was about to devour it. The cement steps leading up to the porch were so badly cracked I had to step carefully to avoid tripping. Dr. Kestler obviously had put more time into the upkeep of his car than his home.

A heavyset woman wearing an apron opened the door before I even had a chance to knock.

I blinked at the woman, startled by her sudden appearance. "Uh, Mrs. Kestler? We're Cadets McCully and Marshall. We're here to…"

"I'm Mrs. Gunther, Dr. Kestler's housekeeper." She glared at us as if she'd rather let a rat into the house. "Dr. Kestler's expecting you. Follow me."

Blushing at my mistake, I tried to recover quickly. "I'm sorry, Mrs. Gunther, I didn't…"

It was too late. She'd already started down a long hallway to the left of the foyer.

Quickly, Matt closed the front door behind us and we hurried after her. Our footsteps on the bare wood floor echoed against the equally bare walls of the hallway. Thick dust coated the woodwork and old cobwebs clung to the corners of the ceiling.

*What exactly does Mrs. Gunther do here?*

When we reached a heavy oak door at the end of the hall, she opened it and stood there scowling at us as we passed. She closed it behind us and her heavy footsteps echoed down the barren hallway.

The study was as filled with personality as the hallway had lacked it. Matt was right, Dr. Kestler sure did seem eccentric. Everything around me looked like it had come from a museum. The floor to ceiling bookshelves seemed to absorb all the light from the few candles scattered around the room. A thin man with slightly

# A Tragic Introduction

graying brown hair stood from behind a thick mahogany desk and stepped toward us.

"Good afternoon, boys," he said, his voice timid and thoughtful. "In case you haven't guessed, I'm Dr. Kestler."

"Cadet McCully, sir." I smiled as I shook the scientist's offered hand. I had a feeling I was going to like my tutor, no matter how little I liked his housekeeper.

"Cadet Marshall, sir," Matt said, repeating the gesture.

"Superintendent Hinkly told me you two have been struggling in physics." Dr. Kestler led us to a table at one side of the room and motioned for us to take a seat. "I haven't been taking very many students lately. I've been too busy with my inventions."

"Inventions? What do you invent?" I hoped the question sounded like normal curiosity. If I was lucky, I could steer the topic to my parents. If I was extra lucky, I might be able to wiggle one of the transmitter's out of my pocket into the seat cushion while he was talking.

"Something the government wanted to get a hold of." Dr. Kestler's eyes flashed. "They wouldn't let me study in peace. They wanted to protect me. Do I look like I need protection?"

Matt and I looked at him and then at each other. Dr. Kestler wasn't *that* old, but he was as thin as a rail. I doubted he could stand up to much of anyone, but I certainly didn't wish to tell him that.

"A lot of good they did." Dr. Kestler slammed his fist into the desk and made an old-fashioned inkwell jump. "Once their agents were killed, my invention was still stolen."

Now we're getting somewhere!

"Someone was killed?" I hoped I sounded surprised, but my heart was pounding so loudly I could barely hear my own words.

"The government sent their best agents to protect me. McKinny, McCollie – something like that." Dr. Kestler narrowed his eyes and looked at me. "What did you say your name was again?"

I froze and glanced to Matt. *Am I going to blow it on our first day?*

Fortunately, Dr. Kestler didn't wait for a reply. "When their plane crashed one day, everything fell apart."

*You got that right.* I thought ruefully.

"But you boys aren't here to talk about my problems." Dr. Kestler sighed and gave us a toothy grin. "You're here to talk about science!"

Matt and I groaned as Dr. Kestler pulled his desk chair up to the table and began the session.

When we finished tutoring and returned to our dormitory that evening, we found the halls deserted.

"Everybody must be in their rooms studying," Matt commented as we came to our room.

"Which is what we need to be doing, unless we want to be tutored in the rest of our classes." I grinned as I turned the knob and pushed open the door.

# A Tragic Introduction

My grin faded when I saw Winston sitting on the end of my bed.

"What are you doing in here?" Matt pushed past me into the room.

"The door wasn't locked." Winston sneered, standing to his feet. "I heard you two were out getting tutored, but I know better."

"Where do you *think* we've been all afternoon, then?" I asked calmly, determined not to let Winston under my skin.

"I *know* exactly what you've been up to." Winston jabbed his finger into my chest. "You guys are covering for your investigation. Do you think that man is a mad scientist?"

While I was pretty sure Winston didn't have any real idea what we were doing, I didn't like being poked by his bony finger. Roughly, I moved his hand away. "You're nuts."

"Did you find any nuclear weapons in his basement?" Winston continued sarcastically.

"Matt!" I slapped the palm of my hand to my forehead and turned to Matt. "That's where we forgot to look!"

"I'm not joking about this." Winston stomped his foot impatiently.

"Dr. Kestler is tutoring us in physics." Irritation crept into my voice. I was really thankful that we had a reason for being there; I didn't want to lie, even to Winston.

"A cover for your real activities," Winston insisted.

"Are you suggesting that we don't need it?" Matt's voice rose and his face was red. "Maybe you think we're faking our bad grades in physics, too!"

"Never mind, Matt." We didn't need to account for our actions, especially not to Winston. "Winston is done here."

I grabbed Winston by one arm and nodded to Matt to take his other. Together we half dragged, half carried Winston to the door and dumped him in the hall.

"I'm going to Superintendent Hinkly," Winston shrieked as he stood and made a great show of straightening his uniform. "You two think you have everyone fooled, but once I get done talking to him, you'll both be in big trouble!"

Matt slammed the door shut in the middle of Winston's tirade. "Man, I thought we'd never get rid of him!"

"Do you think he really suspects?" I asked softly in case Winston was trying to listen from the hall. I sat down on the foot of my bed. "Or do you think he's just being obnoxious?"

"Either way, we need to be extra careful." Matt sat next to me, his face etched with concern. "He could blow our cover."

"I hope Superintendent Hinkly can calm him down." I shook my head in frustration. "Even if he does, we're still going to have to keep an eye out for that jerk

# A Tragic Introduction

following us. He's never going to rest until he can get something on us."

"Another thing to worry about," Matt grumbled, "on top of everything else."

"We can't worry about him now." I rose to my feet and walked to my desk. Winston was nothing more than a serious pain. "Right now we need to be worrying about our homework."

Matt and I had been working on our homework for nearly an hour when the door came swinging open again. A furious Winston stomped into the room.

"So." I turned in my desk chair to face Winston. His face was beet red. I covered a smirk as I asked, "How did it go?"

"He wouldn't even listen to me!" Winston's whiny voice rose an octave. "He just repeated what you guys said and told me I should mind my own business."

"Sounds like a good idea." I turned back to my desk so Winston couldn't see the smile on my face. "Maybe you should listen."

"For once," Matt muttered, never taking his eyes off his work.

"I'm making this my business!" Winston shouted. "I'll find out what you two are really up to. When I do, you'll be sorry!"

Winston stormed back into the hall, slamming the door behind him.

"I think we've made ourselves an enemy." I commented to Matt wryly.

## Jessica C. Joiner

"You think?" Matt snorted as he rolled his eyes.

Somehow, in light of everything else going on in my life, having an eleventh grade bully on our tails seemed relatively unimportant. It wasn't like Winston was going to get us killed or something, right?

# Chapter

Tuesday passed uneventfully. We kept our distance from Winston, though he did seem to be following us the whole day. Dr. Kestler kept us so busy with tutoring that we were unable to learn anything new there. Wednesday, after morning classes were over, Matt and I walked to the General Washington Student Commons for lunch.

As we sat down at a table and paused to say grace, I added silently, *Protect my parents, Lord, where ever they are. Help us to find them soon.*

I opened my eyes with a sigh and saw Trinity standing across from me.

# Jessica C. Joiner

"Mind if I join you?" she asked with a smile.

"Go ahead." I smiled back, motioning with my hand to the spot across from me. I couldn't help noticing that she managed to look great even in her Academy uniform, then remembered Matt's teasing and lowered my gaze to my plate.

"Uggh." Trinity made a face as she sat down. "I am so tired of Winston. He had the audacity to tell me that I was just like my mom. He knows *nothing* about my mom!"

Somehow in the short time he had been at the Academy, Winston had managed to learn exactly what bothered each student the most. Trinity couldn't remember her mom, but she also couldn't forgive her for leaving her and her dad when she was young. Comparing Trinity to her mom was probably the worst insult Winston could have given her.

"So what did you say to him?" I asked.

"Nothing!" She slammed her plate down in front of her. A few of her potato chips bounced off and scattered across the table. "But only because we were already in class. If it weren't for the teacher, none of the other student would have stopped me. They're as tired of him as I am."

"Join the club." Matt rolled his eyes and took a large bite out of his ham sandwich.

"The teachers love him." I allowed just a hint of the frustration I felt into my voice. "They just think he's having trouble 'adjusting to his peer group.' He's doing

# A Tragic Introduction

great in all of his classes. They act like he's some sort of genius."

"He's a genius at getting other people to do his homework for him," Trinity said, lowering her voice. "But none of his victims are willing to talk."

"Perhaps your dad could help?" I suggested. Coach Shiloah had no tolerance for cheaters, and little reason to care for Winston, especially after his behavior at the game.

"I'm going to talk to him about it tonight. Maybe he can do something." Trinity glared down into her glass. "I wish Winston had never transferred here."

"At least we don't have to see him in the afternoon," I commented, popping a potato chip in my mouth.

"Yet another great reason for tutoring." Matt smiled sweetly at Winston, who was watching us from a couple tables away.

Winston glared back at him, pointed two fingers at his own eyes, and then at Matt to signal, "I'm watching you."

"You know, we could always swing by after tutoring today and pick you up for church tonight." I finished my sandwich and tried to cover my nervousness as I looked at her. "I'll pay for dinner."

She hesitated for just a moment, as if considering my offer. "Church isn't really my thing, Scott, you know that." Her blue eyes twinkled mischievously. "But if you ever want to buy me dinner any other time, I might be willing to say yes."

Matt coughed beside me as my ears burned red.

"Ummm... I'll keep that in mind." *Ugh.* Even I knew that was incredibly lame.

Fortunately, Trinity just laughed at my awkwardness as we stood to clear our plates.

The rest of the school day was fine. I mean, Winston eventually ignored us in favor of irritating other students and I managed not to stuff my foot in my mouth again. Once our last class was over, Matt and I raced to our room to prepare for tutoring and church.

"We'll have to leave straight from Dr. Kestler's." I pushed open the door to our room. "You'll want to make sure you have your – What happened in here?"

The room looked like it had been trashed. Dresser drawers had been removed and their contents strewn over the room. Bookshelves had been roughly emptied and books lay in piles, open and bent. Our laundry hampers had been dumped and the dirty clothes had been mixed with the clean clothes so that I could no longer tell the difference. The sheets had even been ripped off our beds.

"Winston!" Matt growled as he waded through a pile of junk into the room.

"When would he have had time to do this?" I waved my hand at the mess. "He was in school the same as us."

# A Tragic Introduction

"He's not in all the same classes as us, maybe he skipped class to try to figure out what we're doing." He bent to gather his scattered comic book collection and glared at a creased cover. "Besides, who else could it have been?"

"Not a teen." My voice was low as I tried to keep my suspicions from turning to fear. "What teen would think to pull the blinds off the windows or shove the mattresses off the beds?"

Matt laid his pile of comics on his desk and looked at the room again. "That's a scary thought. How would they get in?"

"We got out," I reminded him as I sat on the floor next to a pile of clothes and began to try sort out the clean ones and fold them.

Matt picked up a few textbooks thoughtfully before responding. "Do you think anything's missing?" He frowned. "We don't have anything worth taking, so why else would they do this?"

"To scare us?" I suggested, although I was really more irritated than scared. I paused to sniff a shirt I had picked up and made a face as I sorted it into the "Dirty" pile. "To find out if we're working with SATURN? I'm not sure."

I looked at the mounds of scattered things and sighed. "I am sure we're not going to get to Dr. Kestler's this afternoon. This is going to take a while."

# Jessica C. Joiner

"Do you think we should tell Chris?" Matt gave me a glare that made his preferred answer to that question clear.

I paused for a moment to take a pile of dirty laundry to the hamper before answering.

"No," I said slowly. "Not unless something's missing. Superintendent Hinkly will insist it was just another student, and we can't prove otherwise. We'll just need to make sure we lock the door when we leave."

"Are you sure we can't just stuff this mess under the bed and clean it up later?" Matt groaned as he looked at how much we had left.

I just stared at him.

"Guess not."

We finished picking up just in time to get ready for evening formation at 1800. As soon as formation was over, we grabbed a bite to eat and hurried out to my car. We had permanent passes to leave the campus on Wednesday evenings, as long as we drove directly to church and came directly back. While the school wasn't in any way religious, Superintendent Hinkly had a great respect for the part religion played in the founding of our country and allowed any of the students to worship as they pleased.

"If it was an intruder," Matt began as I turned the car onto the road. "Why us? As far as anyone knows, we're just two high school students being tutored in science."

## A Tragic Introduction

"I don't know." I'd been asking myself the same question. "Maybe they just wanted to be sure, or maybe we slipped up somehow."

"I can't think of how," Matt said skeptically. "We haven't done anything unusual."

"I've been running the last few days over in my head," I said as the church came into view. "I can't think of anything we might have done wrong."

I pulled into the west parking lot of Faith Community Church. It was a large church on the outskirts of Baltimore. The building was new but still had a quiet, traditional look to it. Matt and his brother began attending Faith when they had moved to the Baltimore area. He had invited me to come the first week of my freshman year. It was a bit bigger than what I was used to, but I became used to the size fairly quickly.

"Well, don't worry about the mess." Matt unbuckled his seat belt and stepped out of the car. "It's cleaned up now, and you won't be able to concentrate on Preacher's message if you keep thinking about it."

"I'll do my best," I promised as we walked through the church's double-hung glass doors and entered the auditorium, although I wasn't sure how good my best would be.

Five rows of red, upholstered pews fanned away from the platform at the front. We headed down the aisle just left of the center row and went straight to our usual pew, about three from the front on the left, and sat down. The service was just about to begin.

# Jessica C. Joiner

The music director stepped up to the pulpit to begin the service. "Please turn in your hymnal to hymn 325, 'Trust and Obey'"

Mechanically, I stood to my seat and began to sing the words to the familiar hymn, but my mind was already far away.

*I wonder if we did slip up. Perhaps someone saw us talking to Chris or Mr. Jackson.*

The song ended and the music director instructed the congregation to be seated. I continued following the order of service with my body, but not with my brain, until Pastor Williams got up to speak.

"Turn in your Bible to the book of Job." The preacher's voice broke into my thoughts.

*You really don't believe in coincidences, do you , God?* My conversation with Trinity came to mind. God has a way of using others to remind us of stuff we probably should have remembered on our own. *I really do feel like Job right now.*

Suddenly I was overwhelmed by memories of my parents. They felt church was important. They felt God was important. Even when they were on one of their "business trips," they'd always made sure my babysitter took me to church. Pictures of them ran through my mind like a slide show. Each memory brought another and another until I felt like I was about to be overwhelmed by emotion.

I swallowed a lump rising in my throat and forced my runaway thoughts to a grinding halt. *Dear God, please*

# A Tragic Introduction

*be with them, wherever they are. They love you, Lord, and I know
you love them. Please protect them.*

"Point number three: Job Trusted in God." The
preacher's voice again broke into my thoughts. "Look at
chapter thirteen, verse fifteen. 'Though He slay me, yet
will I trust in him.'"

*Oh, man!* I frantically tried to find the verse the
preacher was reading. *I've missed over half the message. I've got
to start paying attention!*

Almost as soon as I had found my place, my
distracted mind strayed again. I probably heard the last
half of the message about as well as I had heard the first
half. Memories of my parents consumed my thoughts.

As Matt and I drove back to the Academy after
the service, Matt commented, "That was a great message,
wasn't it?"

"Huh?" I asked, glancing up from the moonlit
road. My mind was still far away. "Yeah, I guess it was."

"Did you even hear any of it?" Matt asked
suspiciously.

"It was out of Job," I offered weakly.

"What chapter in Job?"

"I don't know. That's about all I heard," I
admitted with a sigh. "I kept thinking about my parents.

"I know." Matt laid a sympathetic hand on my
shoulder. "We'll find them."

I stared silently at the road for a moment and
then glanced out my rear-view mirror. "Man, that guy is
right on our bumper." I was trying desperately to stop

thinking about my parents, even if it meant focusing on something as minor as a lousy driver behind me.

"Maybe it's Winston," Matt joked.

"Matt." I laughed, relieved at the change in subject. "Winston's not to blame for everything."

"Sure he is." Matt tucked his arms behind his head and grinned. "Everything can be traced back to him. I'll bet the hole in the ozone layer was caused by all his hot air."

"You're hopeless…"

I broke off as my car lurched forward.

"What was that?" Matt gasped, grabbing at the dashboard.

"That guy back there just rammed us!" I clenched my teeth as I fought to keep the car from hitting the steel guardrail between us and a deep ditch to our right. I was thankful that my car was old and bulky. I felt better knowing there was a lot of metal between us and that guardrail.

Metal shrieked against metal as the car hit us again, sending us careening into the guardrail in spite of my efforts.

Sweat ran down my face as I pulled the car back onto the road. "Start praying, Matt. That's the end of the guardrail. If he hits us again, we'll be in the ditch!"

"What do you think I've been doing?" Matt snapped back, gripping the dashboard with white-knuckled hands.

# A Tragic Introduction

Stars flashed in my eyes as the jolt from the third hit slammed my head into the steering wheel. I lost control of the car, sending it skidding into the ditch. My head bashed against the window as the car jerked to a stop. An engine roared beside us as the car that hit us sped down the road into the darkness.

"Scott?" Matt shook my arm, his voice filled with concern. "Are you all right?"

"I'll be fine." I groaned, touching the bump on my forehead gingerly. *How am I going to explain this back at school. If my car can even get us back to school.* Another bump was growing on the side of my head where I had hit the window, but that, at least, would be covered by my hair. "Let's get out and look at the damage."

We stepped out of the car and looked it over. A nearby streetlight allowed us to see fairly well. The rear bumper was crumpled and a long gash had been scraped in the already peeling paint on the passenger's side.

"It doesn't look much worse than it did before." I grinned weakly as I traced the gash with my fingers. Another dent or scratch on my battered car would blend right in.

"It could have been much worse." Matt face was practically white in the light of the street lamp. "We could have been killed!"

"I don't think whoever was driving that car was trying to kill us," I reasoned as I climbed back in the car. "I think he was trying to scare us. It was probably the same guy who wrecked our room."

"I think we need to call the police," Matt said as he sat down and closed the car door, "or at least call Chris."

"And get pulled off the case?" I backed the car out of the ditch and on to the road. Matt was probably right, but I was not about to lose my only chance to find my parents. "We're not hurt, and my car looked like it had been in an accident already."

"What about your head?" Matt argued.

"Just a couple of bumps, probably just a bruise. Nothing serious." I had to convince Matt it was no big deal. "Please, Matt. We'll just have to be more careful, that's all."

"Fine," Matt conceded reluctantly. "I know how important staying on this case is to you, but from now on, if anyone so much as looks at us funny, we're going to Chris."

# Chapter

The next morning, I carefully avoided contact with anyone who might ask about my forehead, including Trinity. The bump had risen to a nice blue and purple goose egg that seemed impossible not to notice. A couple of my teachers looked at me funny, but I ducked in and out of class so fast that none of them had time to ask me about it. I was really thankful when Matt and I finally headed to Dr. Kestler's for our tutoring. Thankful, but also edgy.

"Some secret agents we've turned out to be." I hit the steering wheel with the heel of my hand. "We've only been at this a couple of days, but we've already managed to blow our cover."

"We don't know that." Matt didn't sound very convinced.

"Right. Because teens like us get our dorm rooms trashed and our cars shoved off the road all the time." Sarcasm covered my fear. We were in over our heads.

"Call. Chris." Matt rolled his eyes and leaned toward me. "He's trained for this. We're not."

"And get pulled off the case? Maybe sent to my grandparents' ranch?" I gripped the wheel harder as the fear I was fighting crept into my voice. "SATURN doesn't even believe my parents are alive."

"Chris does."

"He told you that?" This was news to me. I couldn't get Chris to give me the time of day.

"He didn't have to." Matt scoffed. "You saw the way he acted around Mr. Jackson. They don't agree about what happened to your parents, and I know my brother well enough to know he won't be happy until he knows for sure."

I had noticed Chris's odd behavior, too. Perhaps it was time to pin Chris down on exactly how much he knew about my parents. "I'll call him as soon as we get to the dorm."

"Did you get all the bugs planted?" Matt asked softly as we pulled into Kestler's driveway.

## A Tragic Introduction

"All but one." I dug a tiny disk from my pants pocket and handed it to Matt. "I figured you could plant it in his car, since you were admiring it so much."

An eager grin split Matt's face as he took the bug from my hand. He'd only stared at the car every day we'd come, even gotten up the courage to caress the flawless black paint on the hood of the ancient vehicle. I wasn't even sure the thing could drive, but it seemed worth the risk.

Matt stepped from my car and crossed to the Model T, admiring it the same way he'd done the day before. I followed a few steps behind, partly to shield him from view of the house and partly to keep myself from looking like a nervous idiot while I waited for him.

Maybe spy genes run in the family after all – in Matt's family at least. I didn't even see him plant the bug, and I was watching for it.

When he stepped back from the car, a mischievous smirk lit his face. "How much trouble do you think I'd get into if I sat in it, just for a moment?"

"Do you want to get us kicked out of here, too?" I shoved his shoulder playfully.

"Because that's exactly what would happen." Mrs. Gunther's voice behind us made me jump.

I held my breath and hoped the guilt on my face looked normal for a teen caught horsing around an antique car.

"If you punks have so much as scratched Dr. Kestler's car, I'll make sure you pay." She stepped down from the porch and crossed the yard to us menacingly.

# Jessica C. Joiner

My eyes went wide as I instinctively took a step back – right into the Model T. I winced as her glare deepened.

"Good afternoon, Mrs. Gunther." I swallowed hard and extended my hand as I stepped away from the car. "How are you today?"

"Dr. Kestler is waiting for you." She ignored my hand and scowled past me at the car. "You'd better not keep him waiting any longer."

With a quick nod, I circled past her into the house with Matt close behind. She stayed back and muttered angrily to herself as she buffed at an invisible scuff on the car with her apron.

As soon as we were inside, Matt whispered, "Do you think she suspects, or does she just hate everyone?"

"I don't know." I sighed. "Are you sure you hid *it* well enough?" If she found that bug, we were toast.

"Well enough." Matt sounded a little doubtful, which didn't help me feel better. "Please tell me I'm not the only one who would hate to do this for a living."

"No kidding." I laughed as I knocked on the heavy oak door at the end of the hall. *How do my parents and Chris do this all the time?*

"Come in," a voice muffled by the thick door answered.

Every time we entered Dr. Kestler's study, it felt like we were going back in time to a Victorian drawing room, complete with candlelight. The eccentric scientist

# A Tragic Introduction

seemed to prefer candlelight to light bulbs. I hadn't seen a light bulb anywhere.

*No wonder. If his experiments went wrong, at least he wouldn't be in the dark.*

Dr. Kestler sat, his brow furrowed, staring at a stack of papers in his hands. As we entered, he started, as if he'd already forgotten we were there, and hurriedly stuffed the papers under a folder on his desk.

"Boys. Welcome." He cleared his throat and pushed his glasses up his nose. "Please, take a seat."

I walked close to Dr. Kestler's desk as I headed to the table. hoping to get a glimpse of what he was working on. Half of a page stuck out from beneath the folder.

… only son of Eric and Marisa McCully, agents of the Secret Agent Training and Reconnaissance Network…

A sharp breath caught in my throat. How long had he known? And if he knew, who else knew about us?

Matt met my gaze as we sat at the table and opened our books. He gave a short nod toward the incriminating papers and clenched his jaw.

"I saw," I whispered. Like it or not, Chris needed to know our cover was blown.

"Turn in your textbooks to page seventy-six." Dr. Kestler tapped the tip of his bony finger on the table between our text books. "Your grades won't improve if you don't take this seriously. That *is* why you're here isn't it?"

"Nobody who's seen my last test grade would ask that question," I quipped, then bit back a nervous laugh. Maybe I was a lousy spy, but I wasn't going to start lying now.

Matt gave me half an appreciative grin as he thumbed through his textbook.

Dr. Kestler's only response was a narrow look and a soft "harrumph." I doubt he was convinced, but at least he stopped asking questions.

I'd like to say I learned a lot from that lesson, especially knowing it would likely be our last after I told Chris what we found, but I was too concerned about what exactly was in those papers to concentrate. Even Matt glanced back at the desk several times when Dr. Kestler wasn't looking.

"Good work, boys." Dr. Kestler finally ended his lesson and followed us to the door of his study. "Do remember stop by the kitchen before you go. Mrs. Gunther said she would have a snack ready for you."

Matt and I looked at each other warily as Dr. Kestler closed the door behind us.

"An apology for how unwelcoming she's been?" Matt suggested.

"Or a chance to really grill us." I took a deep breath and straightened my back. "Do you think she's read those papers, too?"

"*I'd* like to read those papers," Matt grumbled. "Do you think there's one on me?"

# A Tragic Introduction

"It's a safe bet." I shook my head and started down the hall. "Maybe if we play this right, we can find out exactly how much they do know."

We followed the warm scent of freshly baked chocolate chip cookies to the open kitchen door. The kitchen was industrial looking and uninviting, and my own apprehension didn't help the atmosphere.

"Come on in, boys." Mrs. Gunther looked like her face would crack if she smiled any wider. "I've made chocolate chip cookies just for you."

The small table in the center of the spotless kitchen was set with two glasses of milk and two plates of steaming cookies.

"Thank you, ma'am." I took a seat and was swiftly echoed by Matt, who sat down opposite me.

Mrs. Gunther stared at us awkwardly as we prayed for our snack, then blurted, "Tell me about yourselves."

There it was. *Give me the wisdom not to make this worse than it already is.* "What would you like to know?"

"Who are you? Where did you come from? Why are you here?"

"I'm Cadet Scott McCully," I answered readily. She already knew that much. "And this is Cadet Matthew Marshall. We're students from John Jay Military Academy, being tutored in Physics by Dr. Kestler."

"Why are you *here*?"

"I didn't pick the tutor." I dipped a cookie in my glass of milk. "You could call the school and ask them if you like."

"Either of you ever heard of SATURN?"

"Sure," I answered easily.

Matt's foot smacked into my left shin under the table. I blinked twice and ground my teeth to keep from wincing. Or kicking him back.

"It's one of the nine planets in our solar system," I continued naively. "The one with all the rings."

I stuffed the milk-soaked cookie into my mouth and reached for another as I fought to hold back a grin. I had definitely won that round.

Angrily, Mrs. Gunther stormed out of the kitchen. As soon as she was out of sight, Matt let out a long breath.

"Man, Scott," he whispered. "I thought you were going to give us away for sure!"

"We must have already given ourselves away somehow," I said as I rubbed my leg where Matt had kicked me. "Why else would she ask that? And why the profiles on us?"

"Maybe they're just paranoid enough after all that's happened to run some sort of background check on us." Matt yawned widely.

"On teens? Besides, what kind of background check would turn up our SATURN connection?" I covered my own yawn with my hand. "You know, Matt, I think you're contagious."

My head felt like it was stuffed with cotton balls. I shook it to clear it, but I only got more groggy.

# A Tragic Introduction

"Matt?" It was as if I hadn't slept in a week. "Are you as sleepy as I…"

I stopped. Matt had folded his arms on the table and rested his head on them. He was beginning to snore softly.

*What in the world!* My head drooped heavily. *It's as if we've been…*

I jerked my head up. *Drugged!* I tried to stand, but my knees buckled, and I to the floor beside my chair.

*Was she the one after Dr. Kestler all along?* I couldn't keep my eyes open. *We've failed. SATURN was counting on us. Chris was counting on us…*

My whole world was slipping into a heavy black fog. Mom and Dad were counting on us… And I'd managed to fail them all.

# Chapter

"Scott? Wake up, Scott," a voice called faintly from somewhere in the darkness.

I opened my eyes slowly and stared blankly at the source of the voice. The darkness was gone now, but room blurred and spun in front of me. I also had a headache that rivaled the one I'd gotten when Winston hit me.

"Come on, Scott," the voice spoke again. It sounded suspiciously like Chris.

## Jessica C. Joiner

I moaned and blinked, trying to force my eyes to focus on the figure standing over me. I was lying on the kitchen floor at Dr. Kestler's house.

"Chris?" I slurred as I sat up shakily. "How'd you get here?

"When you two didn't show up back at school, Superintendent Hinkly got concerned and called me." He looked a little relieved to see me awake. "What happened?"

"We blew our cover." I struggled to climb back into my chair, but my rubbery legs wouldn't cooperate. Only Chris's quick reflexes kept me from ending up on the floor again. He helped me take a seat beside Matt, who was still sitting in his chair with a dazed expression on his face. "Dr. Kestler had a file on me that included information about my parents' true job. Sorry, Chris we messed up somewhere."

"No, I messed up by not providing you with better back up." Chris responded dryly, "And you can blame your friend Winston for blowing your cover."

"Winston!" Matt's dark eyes flashed. "What does he have to do with this?"

"Superintendent Hinkly overheard Winston bragging about doing some investigating of his own." Chris spun a chair around and sat in it backwards facing us.

"What does that mean?" Maybe I should have let Matt knock Winston's block off.

# A Tragic Introduction

"Winston said that he had been asking Mrs. Gunther questions about you two. Winston didn't seem to have learned anything, but I guess Mrs. Gunther got suspicious enough to have you investigated."

"He could have gotten us killed!" Matt pounded his fist in the table.

"Wait, if Mrs. Gunther drugged us, was Dr. Kestler in on it, too?" I glanced around the kitchen and into the hall. The only people I could see were dressed like Chris. "Is she still here?"

"No one is here." Chris's voice was soft and his expression was hard and unreadable. "Dr. Kestler's study has been ransacked and signs of a struggle indicate he was kidnapped."

I groaned and slumped down in my chair. Now whoever took Dr. Kestler's weapon had Dr. Kestler as well.

"We believe Mrs. Gunther's suspicions forced her hand. She drugged you boys to give her time to get Kestler out of the house," Mr. Jackson said from the kitchen doorway.

Three years at the Academy had trained me well. I stood to attention quickly, but was forced to sit even more quickly as a wave of dizziness hit me. Matt saw my reaction and stood more slowly.

"We found the bottle of sedatives in the cupboard." Mr. Jackson nodded for Matt to sit and set a pill bottle on the table. "Once you two were out, she carried Kestler off in his car."

"But why would she kidnap him?" Matt asked. "I though he hired her."

"We're not sure yet," Mr. Jackson replied. "Probably she was paid off by the people behind the McCullys' deaths."

"Unfortunately, we still don't know who they are." A deadly look crossed Chris's face and I suddenly was very glad I wasn't one of the guys who'd crashed my dad's plane.

"Dr. Kestler's car? You mean the Model T?" Excitement filled my voice as I looked from Mr. Jackson to Chris. "Matt placed a bug in there this afternoon. Maybe we could..."

"'We' are going to do nothing," Mr. Jackson interrupted.

"What!" I shot to my feet again, tipping my chair over as I did. I grabbed the table to steady myself and blinked away the dizziness. Matt just stared open-mouthed at Mr. Jackson.

"You two are off the case," Mr. Jackson said firmly. "I should never have let you help in the first place."

"Mr. Jackson, you can't do this," I protested. *Not when I was so close!*

Mr. Jackson held up his hand. "Let me finish. I should have known better than to get two teens involved in a case of this magnitude. It's too dangerous; SATURN work needs to be done by trained agents, like Agent Marshall. What if she had used poison?"

# A Tragic Introduction

"What if she had?" I asked quietly, my green eyes flashing angrily. "No one had any reason to suspect her. If she had used poison, Chris would have been just as dead as we would have been. What could he have done differently?"

"Agent Marshall is trained for this sort of thing," Mr. Jackson retorted. "He'd have seen the signs and not taken the poison to begin with."

"You put us on this case because you couldn't use a regular agent," I reminded him, fighting to keep my voice even. He was probably right, but admitting that sealed our dismissal from the case. Besides. I was not about to get in a shouting match with the head of SATURN. "How many of your agents could have come as close as we did?"

"A lot of good it did," Mr. Jackson shot back.

"Can you tell us how many bugs your men were able to place?" Anger flashed in Matt's eyes as he joined me against Mr. Jackson.

"He does have a point, Alan," Chris agreed. His tone was respectful, but the same fire lit his eyes that I'd grown familiar with seeing in Matt's. "We only agreed to use them because we weren't having much success on our own."

"Agent Marshall, you can't seriously be suggesting that was continue to utilize them?" Mr. Jackson gave Chris a look of anger and disbelief.

# Jessica C. Joiner

Before Chris could respond, another SATURN agent entered the room. "Mr. Jackson, sir? I think you need to see this."

Matt and I scrambled after Mr. Jackson and Chris as they followed the agent out into the hall and up a narrow flight of stairs to a sparsely furnished room at the top. Another agent stood at the door waiting for us.

"This is Mrs. Gunther's room," The first agent explained as we entered the room. "We've finished the bedroom and are just getting ready to go over the attached bathroom."

"What have you found so far?" Mr. Jackson asked.

"Plenty," the agent replied, directing Mr. Jackson to a tall oak dresser to one side. "Take a look at this."

The dresser drawers had been pulled out and turned upside down on the floor. Mr. Jackson stooped to examine the drawer the agent pointed out. Taped to the bottom was an envelope addressed to Mrs. Gunther. Instead of a return address, a red rattlesnake was drawn in the left corner. The envelope was open.

"The Snake," Chris whispered hoarsely, his hand drifting to the butt of his gun.

"No wonder the McCullys were targeted." Mr. Jackson looked back to the agent. "Was there a letter?"

"No, sir." The agent shook his head. "She probably removed the contents sometime after she hid the envelope here."

# A Tragic Introduction

"The Snake's involvement raises the stakes considerably." Mr. Jackson stood slowly, his eyes still glued on the envelope.

"If I may, sir." Chris's voice was low and his posture tight like a deadly cat. "If the Snake has Eric and Marisa, time is of the essence."

"Eric and Marisa are *dead*, Agent Marshall." Mr. Jackson whirled to face Chris. "The fact that the Snake is behind this should end any further doubts you have. I've half a mind to bench you if you can't get your head on straight."

Mr. Jackson glanced at Matt and me suddenly, as if he had just realized we were there.

"Agent Marshall," Mr. Jackson spoke quietly to Chris, never taking his eyes off us. "Escort the boys back to the Academy immediately."

"But, Mr. Jackson!" I protested. We'd finally found something, something that not only told us who had my parents, but also indicated that they were in very real danger. I couldn't quit now.

"And tell Superintendent Hinkly to ground them to the campus until I give further orders."

"You can't…" Matt stiffened and took a step forward, but was stopped by a warning glare from his brother.

"It's for your own good." Mr. Jackson's voice allowed no arguments. "This is far more dangerous than I first believed. You two are off the case… for good!"

# Chapter

My heart sank as my last hope for finding out anything about my parents was flushed down the drain.

"Alan." Chris stepped between us and Mr. Jackson. "May I speak to you a moment?"

"You may." Mr. Jackson nodded curtly. "But don't expect…"

"In the hall, please," Chris interrupted, turning toward the door.

Mr. Jackson silently followed Chris into the hall, closing the door behind him.

"What are we going to do now?" Matt whispered as soon as the door was closed. The other agents continued to work on the attached bathroom at the back of the room as if meltdowns like this happened everyday.

"Not give up, no matter what Mr. Jackson thinks." I knew I was being both naive and stubborn. We seriously could have been killed today. We were in way over our heads and risked definite expulsion if we defied Mr. Jackson's orders. "Go back to where we started, I guess, back to the wreck. But I really think that this Snake guy behind Dr. Kestler's kidnapping is probably behind my parents' disappearance also."

"You are aware we could be worse than just expelled, right?" Matt looked down at the red Snake logo and rubbed a hand over his face. "Mr. Jackson's right. This is way too dangerous for teens."

"I won't ask you to help me." I lowered my voice and turned to face the door. I couldn't ask my best friend to give up everything for my problems. "I can handle this alone."

"Absolutely not!" Mr. Jackson's deep voice thundered through the closed door.

"I'll take full responsibility for them." Chris replied just loud enough for us to hear him.

"Scott," Matt whispered, grabbing my arm. "Chris is trying to convince Mr. Jackson to let us stay on the case!"

# A Tragic Introduction

"Pray he succeeds," I returned and put my words to action. If Chris had our backs, perhaps there was hope after all.

"Do you realize what a publicity nightmare it would be if two civilian teens get killed because SATURN put them in a compromising situation?" Mr. Jackson shouted. He didn't seem to care who heard him. "I would lose my job!"

"Nothing will happen to them," Chris assured him, his voice soothing. "I'll make sure of it."

"You can't be sure of anything! Do you want to babysit twenty-four-seven?"

"I'll keep an eye out for them," Chris promised confidently. "You don't think I'd allow anything to happen to my own brother, do you?"

"Give me one – just one! – good reason why I should let you," Mr. Jackson demanded.

I bit my lip anxiously as I strained to hear what was being said. Unfortunately, Chris' answer was too quiet to be heard through the door.

Mr. Jackson's response was not. "What?" he roared so loudly that the door shook.

I took a step closer to the door to be able to hear better and motioned for Matt to join me.

Chris repeated himself, now just barely loud enough to be overheard. "Tehran."

"What is that supposed to mean?" Mr. Jackson asked sharply.

"You owe Eric."

"Killing his only son is no way to repay him," Mr. Jackson returned angrily. "I'm doing Eric a bigger favor by keeping his kid out of trouble."

There was a long pause. It looked like even Chris couldn't convince Mr. Jackson to let us stay on. Unless I wanted to drop out of school my senior year, investigating on my own was out. Perhaps over Christmas break I could do something.

*If Mom and Dad live that long.*

"Clovergate." Chris' voice was soft, as if he regretted having to say the word at all.

Mr. Jackson did not answer.

"You owe me, Alan."

"That's blackmail, Agent Marshall." Mr. Jackson's softer voice only amplified his deadly tone. I remembered Mr. Jackson's threat to pull Chris off the case as well and was glad I wasn't in Chris' place right now.

"Jesus, don't let Chris get fired," Matt breathed beside me.

"If there's any chance the Snake has Eric and Marisa, you have to let me go after them," Chris countered. "You know what the Snake will do to them. You can't risk another Clovergate." His voice was decided. "Pull me from the case; fire me if you have to, but I will go after them either way, even if my brother and Eric's son are the only ones willing to help me."

I held my breath for the answer. *Say yes, please, say yes.*

# A Tragic Introduction

"Have it your way," Mr. Jackson snapped. "But hear me, you are totally responsible for them."

"Agreed."

"As far as SATURN is concerned, you are on your own, I will not sanction their involvement." Mr. Jackson continued. I could almost see him wagging his finger at Chris. "If anything happens to either of them, you will answer to the board of directors."

"Agreed," Chris repeated with a grin in his voice. "Thanks, Alan."

"He did it!" I gave Matt a silent high five as we stepped back away from the door.

Mr. Jackson's heavy footsteps stomped down the hardwood stairs and a moment later Chris opened the door. His sunglasses were on and his lips were a thin line. "Scott, Matt, come with me."

Matt and I followed Chris outside without a word, in spite of the many questions I was dying to ask.

As soon as we were in the yard, Chris turned to us. "You two are now my complete responsibility."

"We know," I admitted sheepishly. "We overheard."

"Mr. Jackson was kind of loud," Matt added quickly.

"Mr. Jackson was 'kind of' mad." Chris smiled ruefully. "But I know him well enough that I knew he'd give in eventually. In spite of his public stand, I'm certain he hopes I'm right about Scott's parents."

"We overheard you say 'Tehran'," I spoke up as the three of us walked toward my car. "What does the capital of Iran have to do with anything?"

Chris hesitated before answering. "Several years back, when Mr. Jackson still commanded a field unit, his team was assigned an intelligence gathering mission in Tehran. Certain people were not pleased that they were there. The mission went sour, and only the quick thinking of a young agent named Eric McCully saved the team, including Mr. Jackson."

"And Clovergate?" Matt asked.

Chris sighed. He stared ahead of him as if he were remembering something painful. "Just something I did to help SATURN. I hate to use it to get my way like that."

"But what does Clovergate mean?" I prodded. Chris seemed to be in the mood to talk, which was rare. I wanted to get as much information as I could.

"Clovergate was the code name of a massive security leak at SATURN headquarters. Agents' covers were blown, raids were spoiled, and agents were killed. I had a part in stopping the leak before they could kill Mr. Jackson and the SATURN board of directors." He shook his head painfully and smiled sadly. "Mr. Jackson owes me a favor. I'm just calling it in."

"Why?" I asked as we stopped beside my car. Chris was staring absently at the fresh gash in the side of my car. I hoped he wouldn't ask about it now.

He turned slowly from examining the from the scrape, frowned at me, but didn't comment. "Why what?"

# A Tragic Introduction

"Why risk your job to keep us on the case?" I'd gathered that his loyalty to my parents was part of the answer, but still, Chris was putting his job on the line to allow us to do something he had forbidden in the first place.

"First," Chris said lightly, "it's not much of a risk. Nothing's going to happen to you and Matt. Besides, Mr. Jackson wouldn't fire me."

"But he said…" Matt looked at his older brother with concern.

"He said what SATURN would have wanted him to say. Alan – Mr. Jackson – is one of my closest friends; he'll do all he can to keep me on at SATURN." Chris grinned as he pulled his glasses off and gestured to me. "Besides, you guys have already shown that you're going to investigate with or without our permission. At least this way, I can keep an eye on you."

I looked down at the ground with chagrin. Chris seemed to have me figured out.

"The second reason is…" Chris toyed with his sunglasses as if considering putting them back on. He finally decided against it and stuck the earpiece back into his collar as he sat lightly on the hood of my car and looked at me. "I know exactly how you feel. My dad was missing in action in Iraq. Matt was too young to realize what was going on. I was thirteen. Mom cried herself to sleep every night when she thought we couldn't hear her. I felt so… helpless…" He paused, staring vacantly at the house. "I just wanted to run out there and find my dad. I even tried to run away, but no airline would sell a thirteen-year-old a ticket to a war zone. Even after Dad came home, I felt guilty I couldn't do more to help him. I want to help you the way no one could help me."

"I remember Dad being gone." Matt's deep voice was barely audible. "I just thought he had gone to war. I never knew."

"You weren't supposed to – neither of us were." Chris shook his head slowly. "I found out on my own, but both Mom and I worked hard to keep you from knowing anything. When Dad finally came home, he didn't want to talk about what had happened to him, so it wasn't brought up again."

"I really appreciate your help," I said "But what about the directors of SATURN? Mr. Jackson said that you would have to answer to them if anything happened to us."

"Don't worry about them." Chris flashed me a reckless smile. "I've been interrogated by them before. I can handle them. Besides," he assured us as he stood, "you're not going to be in any danger. I've got any easy assignment for you. That is, if you're interested."

"Sure." As if anything could keep me away. "Anything, as long as we're still on the case."

"Good, because after paperwork, this assignment is about as boring as working for SATURN gets." Chris winked. "You two are going on a stakeout."

"Just tell us where and when," Matt said excitedly.

"You guys ever heard of the Stellar Diner?"

# A Tragic Introduction

"I think so." I nodded slowly. Some of the other students at the Academy talked about it. "It's a crazy sci-fi movie themed restaurant some of the students at the Academy go to in their spare time."

"Exactly, that's why no one will be suspicious to see you there also."

"We're staking out the Stellar Diner?" Matt crossed his arms over his chest and looked at Chris skeptically.

"The place across the street, actually. The diner will be your base of operations. The place you'll be watching is called Davis Janitorial Supply. It's one of many suspected fronts for the Snake's organization." Chris's eyes rested pointedly on the goose egg on my forehead. "I was actually going to suggest it before you made targets of yourselves, but now you'll have to be extra careful not to be seen."

"What are we looking for?" I asked. A stake out actually seemed more productive than being tutored. At least, as far as finding my parents was concerned.

"Last night two of our agents informed us that Davis Janitorial is expecting a large shipment from a phony group called Clarion Distributors," Chris answered. "We think it may be either Kestler or his weapon. Maybe both."

"And our job is to watch out for the shipment," Matt finished for him.

Chris nodded. "Exactly. If you see anything out of the ordinary, contact me immediately. The diner's a public place, so you'll be safe as long as you don't draw attention to yourselves. Under no circumstances are you to act on your own. Understand?"

"Sir, yes, sir," we both answered crisply.

"The Snake is a very dangerous terrorist. Perhaps one of the most dangerous in the world." Chris stared back at the scrape on my car for a moment, then looked me firmly in the eye. "Your lives depend on your doing exactly as I say."

# Chapter

Early Saturday morning, Matt and I began our stakeout. Because we were in Chris's care, Mr. Jackson had not followed through with his threat to have us grounded to the school grounds. Chris had supplied us with spending money and a cell phone to use to call him. I dressed for comfort in a pair of nice jeans and a faded tee shirt and Matt wore his favorite pair of tattered jeans and a hoodie.

Although we weren't dressed in our uniforms, anyone who saw us would be able to tell that we came from the Academy. Matt carried himself in the erect manner of a military man. His dad had trained him that way long before he came to the Academy, but my posture was the same after only three years of training. I was glad that other Academy students came here so we wouldn't be too noticeable.

The outside of the Stellar Diner was painted blue with a large sign in the shape of a rocket displaying the name of the restaurant above the door. We pushed our way through a glass door. A shrill chirp announced our arrival as we entered the bizarrely decorated diner.

"This place is weird," Matt whispered.

I nodded as I looked around. It was definitely not somewhere I would have chosen to go on my own. The diner was dimly lit with stars projected on the walls and ceiling. Framed posters of sci-fi movies and movie stars adorned the walls. On one wall a huge TV screen was playing the latest Star Wars movie.

"Do you think that TV could be any louder?" Matt grumbled.

I grinned wryly, "Look at it this way. If we sit near the TV, no one can accidentally over hear us."

"The question is can we hear each other?"

"At least the food smells good." I took a deep breath as my stomach growled hungrily. "Mmm. Can you smell the bacon?"

We went to the counter and ordered breakfast from a young woman dressed in a Star Trek uniform. Then we took a seat at a futuristic-looking booth near a window facing Davis Janitorial. We had compromised by taking a booth a little distance away from the TV screen,

## A Tragic Introduction

but close enough to cover our conversations if we spoke softly.

"Do you suppose we'll see anything?" Matt asked as we slid around the oddly shaped table.

I shrugged as I stared out the window at the building across the street. No one seemed to be there yet. "I hope so, but I think it will be a long day. We'd better try to look like we fit in here." Matt gave me a cynical look. I shrugged and then continued. "At least we brought some books with us. It'll look like we're doing homework."

"Have you seen any of these movies?" Matt nodded to the flashy movie posters on the walls around us. "I'm afraid war flicks are more in my line."

"A few," I admitted. My mom enjoyed sci-fi and I'd watched a few movies with her, but I preferred to watch mysteries with my dad. "Not enough to pass off as a true fan. Perhaps we'd do better if one of us takes a turn at the arcade in the back while the other watches the window."

"Right." Matt nodded. "Let's hope the expense money Chris gave us holds out until we're finished."

By late afternoon, nothing suspicious had happened. As far as we could tell, Davis Janitorial Supply did normal business. We were getting a little tired and more than a little bored.

"A dollar seventy-five," Matt said as he stuffed his change back in his pocket. "Between food and the arcade, I'm nearly broke."

# Jessica C. Joiner

"That's just enough to order another large order of fries," I suggested. Between the two of us, we had ordered at least five large fries already.

"Come on, can't we order something else?" Matt groaned. "If I have to look at one more French fry, I'll be spending the rest of the stakeout in the little spaceman's room."

"I don't care what you order," I said and made a face at him. "It's my turn to go to the arcade, so I won't be eating it anyway."

I slouched down in the booth. "I wish something would happen. *I'm* getting tired of shooting aliens. You'd think after spending the whole day playing the same game, I'd at least have a high score."

"Do you think Chris could have been wrong about them?" Matt nodded toward the place across the street.

"Who knows." I slid out of the booth to stretch. "Maybe they're just lying low today."

"I guess." Matt opened the notebook he was supposedly writing science notes in and flipped through several pages alternating between his scrawling handwriting and my crisp block print. "We've written down the descriptions of all sixty-seven customers they've had today."

Matt lowered his voice enough to be covered by the sounds of the movie playing behind us. "No shipments and not a single one of the customers looked like a terrorist."

# A Tragic Introduction

I shook my head and sat back down so I could talk without danger of being overheard. "Some of them have to be innocent customers. Probably most of them are. Maybe Chris could recognize…"

"Scott? Matt?" a feminine voice behind me asked in surprise.

I turned in my seat to face the owner of the familiar voice. "Hi, Trinity."

"I've never seen you two here before. Are you sci-fi fans?" Trinity grinned excitedly.

"Today killed whatever curiosity I ever had in that department," Matt grumbled.

I ground my heel into Matt's foot and answered politely, "Not really. We were told about this place by a friend."

"Isn't it great?" Trinity looked around admiringly.

"She doesn't really want an honest answer, right?" Matt gestured his thumb at a nearby picture of an ooze monster covering a city.

I kicked him under the table, a little bit in revenge for his kicking me earlier in the week, and smiled at Trinity. "Do you come here often?"

"A couple times a week. Grandma drops me off sometimes on days Dad's going to be at the Academy late," Trinity said, shuffling her feet awkwardly. "Hey, after I get some food, can I sit with you two? I've got to ask you about… something."

"Sure," I spoke up before Matt could say anything. Not only did I want an excuse not to have to go back to the arcade, but I also welcomed the chance to spend more time with Trinity.

"Great! I'll be right back."

As soon as Trinity was out of earshot, Matt growled, "What's the idea? This is not a good time for a date. We're on a stakeout. We don't want her around."

"We do unless you want to order more fries," I whispered. "She's a regular here. She'll help us look like we actually belong here. Besides, I want to hear what she wants to talk about."

"Fine, you talk to her, and I'll keep watching." Matt turned his gaze back to the warehouse across the street.

"Scott," he whispered hoarsely without taking his eyes off the window. "Isn't that Mrs. Gunther?"

I risked a quick glance across the street to see Dr. Kestler's housekeeper push open the door. Only she wasn't dressed anything like a housekeeper. Tight black jeans and a short-sleeved navy blouse also revealed that what we thought was flab was actually well defined muscle. As she started through the door, she looked in our direction and paused.

"Don't stare." I focused back on the homework in front of me. *Don't let her see us.* "Act normal."

We concentrated intently on the homework in front of us, even though we had finished it hours ago. From the corner of my eye, I saw Mrs. Gunther turn and enter the building.

# A Tragic Introduction

"Looks like Chris was right about that place after all," Matt commented without looking up. "I'll keep watch while you talk to Trinity."

I nodded, closed my books, and turned my attention to Trinity as she returned with her tray.

*Wow, she looks really great today!* She was wearing black denim pants and a green top. Her locket glittered against her shirt in the flashing lights of the diner and her red hair hung loosely around her shoulders. I blushed when I realized I'd been staring at her.

She seemed too preoccupied to notice, but Matt wasn't. He grinned up at me and shook his head with mock pity. Kicking his leg again seemed overkill, so I just rolled my eyes and focused on Trinity.

"Uhh, have a seat," I said awkwardly, slid toward the window, and motioned for her to sit beside me.

"Thanks." She sat next to me and stared uncomfortably at her plate.

"So... what's your favorite sci-fi movie?" I mean, she had said that she came here often, so she had to have one, right?

"You know," Trinity said, still staring at her plate as if she hadn't heard me. "I thought it would take a miracle to keep you guys from getting expelled. Mr. Hinkly's tough on curfew."

"We can thank God we didn't." I shrugged. *And SATURN, but it's not like I can tell her that.*

"I've been thinking a lot since then." Trinity looked up at me and began playing nervously with her locket. "You guys always talk about God and church and stuff. I guess, well… I just wanted to know what was so great. You two go to church more often than I come here. If it's that much fun, maybe I could go with you next time."

"You're more than welcome to go with us on Sunday." I grinned widely. *Thank you, Lord!*

A smile turned up the corner of Matt's mouth as he continued to pretend to do his homework.

"I'll warn you though," I continued, looking at my gaudy surroundings. "If you're expecting a big show or flashing lights, it's not like that. You really don't go to church just to be entertained."

"Then why go so often?"

"We go to worship God," Matt spoke up, his pen poised over his notebook as he risked a glace away from the window. "Because of what His Son, Jesus, did for us."

"Did for you?" Trinity's eyes widened, then narrowed. "Jesus died nearly two thousand years ago."

"You're right, He did die." I nodded. Even if we didn't see anything more at Davis Janitorial, our time here was now well worth it. "But He didn't stay dead. He rose from the dead. He died to pay for our sins so that we…"

"Sorry to interrupt your sermon, Spy Boy, but no one wants to hear your boring fairy tales."

*Not now, Lord,* I thought, dismayed by the interruption. *I just got started!*

I turned sharply to see Winston sneering at us. *How did we not see* him *come in?*

# A Tragic Introduction

"Buzz off, pest." Trinity flicked a fry at Winston. "No one invited you."

"No, no one invited me," Winston said bitterly, looking accusingly at me. "Maybe that's because you don't want Superintendent Hinkly to know what you are up to."

"Maybe it's because you're a bully and a loud mouth," Matt returned hotly.

"Knock it off, you two," I whispered urgently. We were supposed to be blending in, not getting kicked out. "You're making a scene."

"I don't care!" Winston's voice rose above the noise from the TV. "I don't care if everyone hears me. You two have been playing spies long enough. You probably imagine you're on some sort of stakeout or something!"

"Scott," Matt hissed. He tensed and nodded to the window. Mrs. Gunther was crossing the street toward the diner.

"Winston!" My conversation with Trinity was over. If we didn't all get out of here now, any chance of escaping would be, too. "All of you." I started nudging Trinity out of the booth. "Leave. Now."

"Oh, I'm sorry." Winston crossed his arms over his chest. "Did I blow your cover? Are you afraid some thugs are going to come out of that building across the street and get you?"

"Winston!" Matt stood, bumping into the table and nearly spilling Trinity's glass into her lap. He flexed his muscles and looked down at Winston threateningly. "This isn't a game. Move it!"

"Certainly, Cadet Marshall." Winston grinned wolfishly. "I'm sure Superintendent Hinkly will be greatly interested in your extra-curricular activities."

It was too late. The shrill cheep of the door opening made my heart skip. Mrs. Gunther shoved open the door, glanced around the diner with distaste, and glared in our direction.

"What is going on?" Trinity cried as I shouldered her out of the booth.

"The kitchen?" Matt grabbed Winston by both shoulders and propelled him forward. "There's got to be a back exit."

The crowd had picked up and making our way to the kitchen was like navigating a rave. We finally made it through without knocking over any people or dinner trays.

Mrs. Gunther blocked the door, the butt of a handgun just barely sticking up from her waistband.

"The only place you four are going is with me."

# Chapter

Mrs. Gunther motioned for us to head for the door. I glanced desperately around the diner hoping that someone else had noticed the gun or that I might get someone's attention. Everyone was busy doing their own thing, and not paying the least bit of attention to us.

Matt nodded to Mrs. Gunther as if to ask, "Can we take her?"

I shook my head slightly. Even if we could get her down, she could easily shoot one of us – or someone else in the diner - before we could get her gun away from her.

# Jessica C. Joiner

"We're not going anywhere with you." Trinity put her hands on her hips and shouted. "You wouldn't dare do anything here."

A few of the movie watchers shushed her for interrupting their movie, but just went back to watching it.

I wasn't so sure what Mrs. Gunther would dare to do. The movie was in the middle of a loud laser war and the swirling lights left the room with a surreal feeling. Anybody who did witness what was going on would just think it was some fans goofing off. Besides, Mrs. Gunther had proved how ruthless she was already by drugging Matt and me and kidnapping Dr. Kestler.

Mrs. Gunther's hand slid toward her gun.

"Trinity." I quickly put my hand on Trinity's shoulder. My heart was pounding hard against my chest. "Don't test her!"

"That's right." Mrs. Gunther chuckled gruffly. "Just ask your boyfriend what I dare to do. Out the front door, all of you."

"But- but, I'm not with them, honest!" Winston whined, putting his hands up in front of him. "I don't even like them."

"I don't like them either. Keep moving." Mrs. Gunther backtracked to our table and picked up the notebook Matt and I had been writing in.

I winced and blew a sigh through my nose. If she looked in that book, there would be no doubt about what we had been up to. Not that there was anything I could

# A Tragic Introduction

do to stop her, or any way I could see to escape her. Leaving the diner with an armed terrorist was stupid, but challenging her could bring danger to everyone in the packed diner.

"Shut up, Winston," I pushed the words through my teeth. "For once, will you just shut up."

Winston glared at me and opened his mouth as if to retort, but as his eyes tracked something behind me, he paled and closed his mouth again.

"You've been busy boys again, haven't you?" Contempt dripped from Mrs. Gunther's voice as she poked me in the side with the barrel of her gun. "The Snake should have let me use poison in those cookies. Don't tempt me to correct that mistake."

A bolt of fear hit me harder than the pain in my ribs.

"Last time. Move, or I'll be content to take only three of you with me."

Not even Winston could miss the meaning of her threat. All four of us obeyed, weaving our way through the busy diner to the front door. Matt tried to appear tough, but fear glowed brightly in his brown eyes, and he looked very pale. Trinity bravely tried to cover her fear with a mask of anger and indignation. Winston looked like he was one more shock away from either passing out or screaming like a baby. My heart raced, but I forced myself to calm down. If we panicked, we would never get out of this mess.

# Jessica C. Joiner

*Dear God, Help us.* Rising panic threatened any attempt I made to think of a way out of this mess. *Help us to escape. Help us to be brave.*

I took a deep breath to relax. And another. It helped, a little. Focusing wasn't quite as difficult, at least. I trusted God to give us an opportunity to escape, but we would have to be on the lookout for it.

As we left the diner, Mrs. Gunther continued to prod me every so often with her pistol. Each time, fear ran up my back like an electrical charge. No one had ever pointed a gun at me before; it was not an experience I ever wanted to repeat.

We crossed the busy street quickly and stood in front of Davis Janitorial Supply. I swallowed hard. Once we were inside, Mrs. Gunther could do anything to us, and no one would know. If only there were a way to let SATURN know where we were!

*If only!* An idea sparked in my head. If I could only drop my wallet in front of the building, perhaps someone would find it and turn it in.

*Right,* or *maybe they'll throw it away after stealing what little money I have left.*

Seeing no better option, and more than willing to risk the two one-dollar bills I had left in my wallet, I slowly slid my hand toward my back pocket. *Please don't let her notice.* The tips of my fingers had just brushed against the smooth leather when Mrs. Gunther jabbed me again – hard. I bit back a cry of pain as I jerked my hand out of my pocket.

# A Tragic Introduction

"Don't even think about it, Spy Boy," she growled. "Try another stunt like that, and I'll shoot all four of you as soon as we get inside!"

I rubbed my ribs where she had poked me. Desperation tightened my throat. If something didn't happen soon, we would have little chance of leaving Davis Janitorial alive. If Mrs. Gunther was part of the group who planted the bomb in my parents' plane, she would have no qualms about killing us, too. I paced my breathing carefully to keep from hyperventilating.

*Dear God, save us!* I repeated over and over in my mind. Partly as a prayer, but partly to help keep myself from thinking about how much trouble we were in.

"I'm not going in there," Winston shrieked when we reached the doors to Davis Janitorial Supply. "What kind of idiot do you think I am?"

"Are you kidding me?" Matt snapped, grabbing Winston by the arm and squeezing tightly. "What part of this is not clear to you? She has a gun, you incredible moron."

Winston hesitated, as he considered the gun still grinding into my ribs. "I'm not the moron, you guys are. This is your mess; I refuse to be involved."

"You're already involved, Whiny." Mrs. Gunther took a threatening step toward Winston, pushing me along with her. I arched my back away as she dug the barrel deeper and pain radiated through my side. "Now go inside or you and your friend gets it here."

"Cadet McCully is certainly not my friend," Winston muttered, but he stopped protesting and opened the door.

The showroom of Davis Janitorial looked like a normal shop, with aisles for chemicals and cleaning equipment filling the large room. A dark-haired young woman with a hard expression stood behind the check-out counter. Mrs. Gunther no longer made any attempt to hide the gun as she led us to the back room, but the girl didn't seem to care. It was as if she saw thugs threatening people with guns every day.

If this was really a terrorist front, she probably did.

Perhaps Winston had been right to refuse to go inside. Now that we were here, we were cut off from any hope of escaping. The same hopelessness I felt began to creep over the others' faces. *Lord, I got them all into this, please help me get them out.*

Mrs. Gunther led us to an elevator at the back of the storeroom, prodded us inside, and hit the "B" button.

"Where are you taking us?" Trinity's voice shook and she clutched her locket tightly in her fist as we all piled into the elevator.

"To see the Snake." Mrs. Gunther grinned an ugly, stiff grin as the elevator doors slid open to reveal a long hallway lined with tightly closed steel doors. She motioned us out of the elevator with her gun. "After you."

"You can't do this to me." Winston balked at the elevator door. "Do you know who my father is?"

# A Tragic Introduction

"I don't care if he's the President of the United States." Mrs. Gunther glared at him. "Even he couldn't get you out of here."

"I have money!" Winston's whine rose to a wail. "Just name your price – anything."

"You can take that up with the Snake." Not taking Winston's bait, Mrs. Gunther snarled at the frightened cadet. She took the gun out of my side and waved it at Winston. "Now shut up."

Winston blanched and glared at me as his kidnapping was somehow my fault. Anger rose up inside me. If anything, our situation was his fault. If he hadn't been too busy making a scene in the diner, we might have had a chance to escape.

My anger faded as guilt rose in its place. Winston had a point. I had gotten them all involved, well, maybe indirectly. Perhaps this *was* really all my fault. I shook off my grim thoughts. Neither blaming myself or getting angry at Winston were going to get us out of here. I needed to focus on a way to escape.

Mrs. Gunther led us to the end of the hall, which intersected with another hall to form a T. I paid careful attention to the way back to the elevator in case an opportunity to escape presented itself. She forced us down the right arm of the "T" to a steel door at the end of the stark, white hall. Keeping her gun pointed at us, she pushed a button on the intercom at the right of the door.

"Gunther here, Boss." She kept her eyes and gun focused on us.

# Jessica C. Joiner

"You have them, then?" A sinister voice crackled over the intercom.

"Yes, sir." Mrs. Gunther gave us a mean smile. "All four of them."

"Bring them in. I wish to speak with them myself."

I bit my lip nervously and glanced at Matt. No matter what we did, we just seemed to get deeper and deeper into trouble. Chris had warned us about the Snake, but Chris wasn't here now, and we were about the face the man who had blown up my parents' plane.

Matt returned my gaze steadily. I could see by the fierce glint in his brown eyes that he was still ready for a fight, in spite of the hopelessness of the situation. I shook my head slightly. We would never survive an outright war in a terrorist's hideout. My still-aching side was a good reminder that they were armed, and we were not.

The steel door swung open silently and Mrs. Gunther prodded us into the dimly lit room. The room was well furnished and decorated like a CEO's office, not at all like what I had expected a terrorist's office to look like. In the movies, they always had guns or exotic decorations all over the place.

I could make out the silhouette of a man sitting behind a large desk, but the dim lighting made it impossible to see his face and made an already frightening situation seem downright freaky.

"Teenagers?" the silhouette hissed angrily. "You bring me teenagers? Don't tell me Agent Marshall wasn't with them at least."

# A Tragic Introduction

"No, sir." Mrs. Gunther pushed me, then Matt, forward with her gun. "These are the two Agent Marshall sent to spy on me at Kestler's."

I stared uneasily at the shadow ahead of us. This wasn't exactly how I'd hoped to find out what had happened to my parents, but perhaps he could tell me more than Chris had.

Fear gripped my stomach. He could, but then he would quite literally have to kill us. He couldn't afford to let us leave here alive.

*Us!* I closed my eyes as guilt briefly replaced my fear. Matt was staring bravely at the Snake, the grim look in his eyes showing that he'd reached the same conclusion I had. Trinity was glaring defiantly, but her hands shook as she fingered her locket. Winston unsuccessfully tried to cover his fear with a thin mask of bravado.

My heart grew cold. Sure, I was afraid to die, but I wasn't afraid of what would happen to me after that - or to Matt either, for that matter. Winston and Trinity on the other hand... *Please, Lord, get us out of here. They're not ready to meet you yet.*

"Does SATURN think I'm a child to be babysat by teens?" The Snake's harsh voice rose wrathfully. "Do they not fear me enough to at least send real agents instead of children?"

His voice softened to a malicious whisper. "Soon they will fear me. The whole world will fear me!"

The Snake looked over us carefully.

"Who are you? How much do you know?" His voice was suddenly sweet and condescending, as if he were talking to preschoolers. "Tell me what I want to know, and I will consider letting you go."

"My name is Winston Daytona the third." Winston stepped up readily. "Of the Boston Daytonas. My dad will pay you well if you return me unharmed."

"Whether you remain unharmed relies entirely on how well you cooperate," the Snake said threateningly.

Matt and I glanced at each other grimly. The Snake wouldn't dare let any of us go now that we knew the location of his hideout. He couldn't risk our reporting to SATURN. Besides, if Matt and I did tell him how much we knew, we could get all of us in even more trouble. Our best bet might be to play dumb and hope we were convincing.

"What's wrong with you?" Trinity shouted at the Snake, her voice laced with panic. She twisted her locket so frantically, I was sure it would break off in her hands. "We are teens, not spies. Teens hang out at that diner all the time. You've made a mistake."

The Snake opened the drawer to the desk and reached inside. With a rasping chuckle, he poured a small pile of shining silver disks on to his desk. "Were these 'mistakes' as well?"

They'd found SATURN's bugs. Matt poked an elbow into my side. We were going to have some trouble talking our way out of that.

"Those two were there all day, writing in this." Mrs. Gunther stepped forward and tossed Matt's notebook on the desk in front of the Snake. "The girl and the short kid met them later."

# A Tragic Introduction

All hope flowed out of me as the Snake thumbed through the notebook silently. Any chance we might have had of passing ourselves off as innocent teenagers was now gone. Matt groaned beside me.

The Snake chuckled menacingly. "Very thorough. You described everyone who came or went from here all day. I'm not sure a real agent could have done a better job."

Trinity stared at us speechlessly.

"The other two had nothing to do with this." Perhaps I could at least persuade him to let Trinity and Winston go. "They were just in the wrong place at the wrong time."

"Yes." The Snake templed his fingers in front of him. "And unless you tell me what I want to know, they will die with you. We'll start with your names. Cadet Daytona here has wisely decided to cooperate." The Snake looked at Trinity. "What about you, young lady?"

"Trinity Marie Shiloh." Her hands dropped to her sides as tears of defeat filled her eyes.

"Good. She, too, realizes things will go easier for her if she cooperates." The Snake turned to Matt. "Your turn."

Matt folded his arms over his chest and spread his feet. The Snake had no reason to recognize Trinity and Winston's names, but if he associated Matt and I with our families, we were all toast.

"Perhaps you need a little reminder. Matthew David Marshall, brother to SATURN Agent Christopher

# Jessica C. Joiner

Marshall." The Snake leaned forward over his desk. "I'm shocked your brother allowed you to get involved, given how the first time he met me turned out."

"Scott *Eric* McCully." The Snake stressed my middle name as he swiveled in his chair to face me. "Only child of SATURN's dynamic duo, the late Eric and Marisa McCully. The same Eric and Marisa McCully that I had killed a week ago?"

*They're not dead!* I fought to keep from reacting as the blood drained from my face. He was just trying to get to me. He had to be.

"SATURN probably told you they died in a plane crash." The Snake chuckled. "Not even SATURN believes that. They only told you that because they thought you could handle it better than the truth."

I wasn't s sure I wanted to know his version of the truth any more.

"I had my men kidnap them, and instructed Mrs. Gunther to crash their plane to cover up their disappearance. The nerve gas was a convincing addition, I thought."

*He's enjoying this.* This was all a game to him, a battle of wits I couldn't afford to lose.

"I had them brought here for interrogation." The Snake paused and glanced at each of us to see the effect his words were having. "I'm afraid our methods were a bit harsh, and your parents were more than a bit stubborn. A body can only take so much."

I stood as pale and stiff as a statue, my eyes staring straight ahead. Winston was silent for once.

# A Tragic Introduction

Trinity cried softly and Matt muttered under his breath angrily, but they sounded very far away. I couldn't move. I felt like I had been kicked in the stomach. *They're not dead. They can't be.*

"I'd like to tell you that they died easily," the Snake said maliciously, "but their deaths were anything but easy. I'm afraid there wasn't even enough left for a proper burial."

*Tortured.* My knees gave out beneath me and I sank to the concrete floor. He was lying, he had to be. *Dear Lord, after all this I can't be too late.* I wanted to scream at the Snake, but the lump in my throat cut off all sound. My eyes burned with blinding tears.

"Take them to the detainment room." The Snake's instructions barely pierced the fog surrounding my brain. "They will be joining his parents soon enough.

# Chapter

Dazed, I followed Mrs. Gunther as she led the four of us back down the long corridor to a steel door with a small barred window. She opened the door to the empty steel-walled room and shoved us inside.

As door clanged shut behind us, I slid down the smooth wall, pulled my knees to my chest, and hid my face in my folded arms, hoping no one noticed as I started crying. Honestly, though, after all that had happened in the past few days, I'm not sure I cared. Matt sat beside me, content to sit quietly until I was ready to talk.

"Tortured." With burning, tear-rimmed eyes, I turned to look at Matt. "He tortured them."

"We all heard," Matt replied. "I'm sorry."

"I don't understand." My stomach didn't hurt any more; I just felt empty inside. "I've been praying for them since I found out about the crash. God could have kept the Snake from killing them. Why didn't He?"

"You can't blame God, Scott." My best friend's voice was filled with worry. "Right now you need to trust Him more than ever. He's the only One who can get us out this mess."

"I know that." I sighed and looked down at my hands. "I trusted Him to save my parents." My voice rose. Even if I didn't *blame* God, He still let this happen. I wasn't sure how I could trust Him now. "He said 'no' to that prayer. How do I know He won't say 'no' to our escaping, too?"

"'Though He slay me, yet will I trust in Him,'" Matt said thoughtfully, more to himself than to me.

"What?" I looked up sharply. I had heard what he said, but I didn't quite catch what he meant by it.

"It's one of the verses the preacher read," Matt said and repeated the verse. "Remember? Job trusted God no matter what happened. If we only trust God when things are easy, what good is our faith?"

I looked back down at my hands. Matt was right, but part of me didn't want to admit that he was. Part of me still wanted to be mad.

# A Tragic Introduction

"We can't do this ourselves," Matt insisted, laying his arm across my shoulders.

"'Though He slay me…'" I took a deep breath and tried to steady my ragged emotions. Matt was right. I was confused and hurt, but I couldn't allow myself to become bitter against God. If I didn't choose to trust Him now, I probably never would. "Pray for me. This isn't going to be easy."

"Pray!" Trinity turned from the corner to look at us with eyes were full of tears and desperation. "Maybe your God could rescue you from Superintendent Hinkly, but this is much worse. Praying won't help us now." Her voice cracked as she turned back to face the corner. "Nothing can help us now."

"Your God couldn't even keep us from getting captured by these wackos," Winston added accusingly. He emphasized "your" as if I were somehow responsible for God's actions.

Matt opened his mouth to retort, but I placed my hand on his arm to stop him. "Leave them alone. They can't trust in Someone they don't believe in. Right now, it's taking all my faith for me to trust."

Matt nodded and looked back at me. "Do you want me to pray?"

"No." Since my personal faith was at stake, this was my responsibility. "I need to talk to God about this myself.

The two of us bowed our heads.

"Dear Heavenly Father." I swallowed back a lump that rose in my throat and pushed on. "Forgive me for not trusting you. Strengthen my faith. Help me to trust you no matter what. Protect us from the Snake and his men and help us to escape. In Jesus' name, amen."

"Amen," Matt echoed and looked over at me. "What's our first step?"

"Getting out of this room." I replied, a wry smile tugging at my lips. *You can step in with that miracle any time, Lord.*

"Great thinking, Sherlock." Trinity turned around to glare at us. "What's our second step? Getting shot down by the guards?"

"Anything's better than waiting for them to come take us for 'questioning.'" Matt offered his hand to help her up. "Are you with us or not?"

Trinity started at his hand for a long time, sighed, and took it reluctantly. "I may not trust your God, but I guess I'll have to trust you guys. I'm in."

"I'm not." Winston snorted. "Cadet McCully got us into this mess. I think we need a new leader to get us out."

"Are you kidding me?" Matt scoffed. "There's no way I'm following a whiny little..."

I ground my heel into the top of Matt's foot. We all needed to focus our energy on getting out of here, not on fighting each other. "Winston, what do you think we should do?"

# A Tragic Introduction

"I think we need to get out of this room," Winston said confidently, as if escaping had been his idea all along. He crossed his arms over his chest and smirked at the rest of us.

"How, genius?" Matt growled, his body tense as he struggled to keep his temper in check.

"Easy, we'll..." A puzzled look crossed Winston's face and then cleared. He gestured to me as if he were a general directing his troops. "A good leader knows how to listen to his men. Cadet McCully, I'm open to your suggestions."

"Fine." I rolled my eyes. At least everyone was calm and thinking. Winston could take credit for everything, so long as we escaped. "We'll need to work together if we are going to pull this off."

I looked at Matt. "We need to get someone out to contact SATURN and bring them down here. Chris has to be worried about us by now."

"Wait a minute," Trinity interrupted. Irritation rose in her voice as she placed her hands on her hips. "Who's SATURN? Don't tell me you guys really are spies!"

"They only think they are," Winston sneered.

"Not really." I shrugged and ignored Winston's jealous barb. "We were just helping out by watching this building. SATURN thought it might be a hideout of some kind. We weren't supposed to be in any danger."

"Do you think Mr. Jackson knows we're missing yet?" Matt asked worriedly.

"I hope not, for Chris's sake." I could just imagine what his reaction would be. "But the longer we're missing, the more likely it is that he'll find out."

"Let's move then." Matt prodded, stretching his arms out in front of him anxiously. "Step one – get out of this room. How?"

"We could try…"

Clang!

The steel door swung open and smashed into the wall, making all of us flinch.

"Scott McCully?" A skinny goon looked right at me as he entered the room. He had a gun in one hand – pointed at me. "The Snake wants you for questioning."

Matt stepped between me and the gun. He pulled himself up to full height and looked down at the smaller guard threateningly. Fear flashed across the guard's face and he gripped the gun with both hands.

"Back off, Matt," I said softly, putting my hand on his shoulder. Fighting a thug with a gun was suicide. There had to be another way

"When I nod," I whispered to Trinity out of the corner of my mouth, keeping my voice low so the guard couldn't hear. We only had one chance. "Pretend to faint. Try to fall against the guard."

Trinity glared at me and whispered back, "I don't faint."

"The Snake has taken a special interest in you, boy." The guard stepped widely around Matt toward me. "I won't hesitate to use force."

## A Tragic Introduction

I opened my mouth to plead with Trinity one last time, but the guard stepped between us and grabbed me by the arm.

I nodded to Trinity anyway, hoping she would do as I had asked.

With the flair of a drama queen, she let out a shrill scream and fell limply against the guard. Knocked off balance, the guard stumbled into me. Matt, locking his hands together, lifted his arms high and smashed his fists down on the guard's head. Stunned, the guard fell, and his gun clattered to the floor at Winston's feet. Winston took a step back as if it would bite him.

I scooped up the gun and pointed it at the guard in case he moved. He didn't. "Nice hit, Matt."

"Thanks, but he won't be down long." Matt rubbed his fist as he looked at the guard critically. "We need to hurry."

I kept the gun trained on the guard while Matt relieved him of his keys. We hurried out to the hall and locked the door behind us. I hoped that would keep the thug's comrades from discovering our escape until the others had a chance to get out of the building.

"Here, Matt." I handed him the gun. "You'll need this to get outside."

"What are you talking about?" Matt snapped, anger and surprise evident in his voice. He jerked his hands away as if I'd offered him a cobra. "You're coming with us."

"Matt," I tried to explain, "this is the Snake's hideout. He's probably holding Dr. Kestler here as well. I won't leave here without finding him." *I won't let him be killed like my parents.* My throat tightened again and I shook off the grim thought.

"I'm not leaving you here to face that nut by yourself," Matt said angrily, pushing the gun back toward me. "If you stay, we all stay!"

"We don't have time to argue about this," I protested. "We might not have much time at all. If you guys can't get outside, SATURN won't make it here in time to save any of us. I'll stay out of sight, honest."

Seeing Matt hesitate, I placed the gun back in his hand. "Hurry, the Snake will begin to wonder what happened to the guard he sent."

"You just want to be the hero," Winston spoke up. "I'm not going to let you take all the glory."

"Whatever," I said quickly before Matt could retort. Winston was going to make it more dangerous for whomever he was with, and I didn't have the time for the long argument I knew it would take to get rid of him. *Let me be making the right choice.*

"Be careful, Scott." Matt handed me the ring of keys he took from the guard and looked at Winston pointedly, but he didn't argue. "I'll be praying."

"So will I." *We'll all need it.*

I watched Matt and Trinity until they reached the elevator at the end of the hall.

*Lord, protect them.* I prayed as the elevator doors slid closed with my friends inside. *Help them to bring SATURN quickly and help me to find Dr...*

# A Tragic Introduction

My prayer was interrupted by the sound of rapid footsteps coming down the hall. There were at least two men coming toward us. The footsteps sounded like they were coming from the left arm of the 'T', the opposite direction of the Snake's office.

*Why'd you stop in the middle of the hall, stupid?* I fumbled with the ring of keys before I found one that would unlock the nearest door, yanked it open, and grabbed the protesting Winston by the arm. Stuffing him inside the tightly packed janitor's closet, I took a deep breath and squeezed in after him. I've hated tight spaces ever since accidentally locking myself in a trunk as a child, but I swallowed my fear as I quietly closed the door in front of me.

The footsteps continued until they were right outside the closet door, where they stopped. Being crammed in the tiny closet made my heart race and forced me to measure my breathing to keep from hyperventilating and tipping off the guys outside. A walkie-talkie crackled and I strained to overhear the conversation.

"What?" Mrs. Gunther answered.

"Veronica says two of the teens escaped." The walkie-talkie crackled again. "The dark-haired boy and the girl just ran past her desk and out the front doors."

*Thank you, Lord.* At least Matt and Trinity were safe.

Winston began to squirm. I dug my elbow into his side to make him keep still. He stifled an angry yelp and elbowed me back, but he stopped moving.

# Jessica C. Joiner

"Why didn't she stop them?" Mrs. Gunther roared. I was glad I wasn't Veronica right now.

"They caught her by surprise," the voice on the walkie-talkie answered. "Besides, they had a gun. They probably took it from Mac when they knocked him out."

Mrs. Gunther cursed loudly. "Get back down here and help find the other two. the Snake will kill us all if we lose the McCullys' brat."

"He may kill us even if we don't," the man with Mrs. Gunther grumbled.

"Shut up," Mrs. Gunther snapped. Steel doors squealed open and slammed closed as the pair started from the elevator and worked their way toward our hiding place.

"We're gonna die. We're gonna die." Winston started whispering, but each time he repeated himself, he got louder. "We're gonna..."

I clapped my hand over his mouth to silence him. I was having a hard enough time trying not to have a panic attack in the small space; listening to him melt down beside me wasn't going to help. On top of that, the overpowering smell of bleach was giving me a headache and the end of a broomstick was jabbing me in the back. I didn't dare move it for fear of making a noise that would attract the thugs looking for me.

The door right next to our hiding place slammed shut. The closet was so tight we couldn't even move enough to hide behind the junk stored in it. I bit my lip hard enough to taste blood. *Lord, we need another miracle.*

# A Tragic Introduction

"Gunther!" a voice called as another set of footsteps came running down the hall. "The Snake has new orders."

"What now?" Mrs. Gunther demanded. "And why didn't he radio them to me himself?"

"He threw his radio against the wall after he heard the teens escaped," the third man replied, his voice trembled with fear. "He says to forget the other two for now. Once the two that escaped get to SATURN, we'll have agents swarming this place. He needs everyone in the garage next to the lab to help load that contraption and the other important stuff onto the trucks."

"What about the McCullys' kid?" Mrs. Gunther sounded reluctant to give up her hunt for me.

"They'll show up eventually." The new thug laughed. "Besides, It's not like the Snake doesn't know how to find the McCully brat when he wants him."

That was not a very comforting thought. Still, I was thankful the attention was off us for now. I waited until the footsteps receded down the hall, let go of Winston, and opened the closet door.

"Some leader you are," Winston complained as he straightened his uniform. "That was positively the worst hiding place ever."

"We survived, didn't we?" I demanded sharply. If he was going to give me any more trouble, I was going to find a way to lock him back in that closet. "No more complaining and no more noise. These men mean business."

"Fine," Winston grumbled sullenly. "What do we do now?"

"We have to get to Dr. Kestler before the Snake's men do." I stared in the direction the men had gone. "We can't let the Snake kill him like he did my parents."

# Chapter

I slipped down the empty hall to the corner of the intersection. Winston followed without protest. The thugs I'd heard outside the closet had mentioned that they were going to the garage next to the lab. If I could find them, I could find the lab. And a lab was the best place to find a kidnapped scientist.

The mental image of my tutor tied to a chair like in the movies, pleading with the Snake to let him go, hurried me down the hall. If Matt and I hadn't been dumb enough to eat drugged cookies, we might have been able to stop his kidnapping in the first place. I wasn't going to let him down again.

# Jessica C. Joiner

Pressing my back against the wall, I peered carefully around the corner to the left just as Mrs. Gunther disappeared through a pair of steel double doors about halfway down the hall. I stuck my arm out to keep Winston from rounding the corner and giving us away. The room she'd entered had to be the garage.

As soon as I was sure Mrs. Gunther was out of sight, I glanced anxiously behind me and down the other arm of the hallway. If we were caught now, Dr. Kestler, Winston, and I would all be toast.

The coast was clear. I tiptoed to the closest door beside the garage, motioning for Winston to follow me.

He complied, with only a deep sigh to show his irritation.

I tried the doorknob as gently as I could. It was locked. The keys Matt had borrowed from the guard opened the door to a storage room. That left the door on the other side of the open garage doors.

*Please let us get by without being seen.* I crept over to the edge of the double doors and paused to listen for the men inside. We had to dash past the doors while the men were too busy to notice us, or we'd be joining Dr. Kestler all right – in captivity.

"Make sure the coast is clear before you cross." I stood right next to Winston's ear and whispered, "We can't afford to be seen."

"Do you think I'm stupid?" Winston growled.

I refrained from answering as I turned back to the doorway. The answer to that question would depend a lot on his actions in the next few minutes.

# A Tragic Introduction

"So where am I supposed to take this stuff?" someone asked from inside. We were running out of time.

Peeking around the doorway ran the risk of being seen, but a quick peek was far better than running by recklessly. I poked my head around the doorway and jerked it back quickly, getting just enough of a glance to locate the people inside. The man speaking was leaning out of the window of a truck cab talking to Mrs. Gunther. Two other men were finishing loading boxes into the truck.

*SATURN would love to know where they're going. I can afford a minute. I hope.* Ignoring the fluttering in my stomach, I flattened myself back against the wall as I listened for Mrs. Gunther's response. Winston nudged me impatiently. I shook my head silently without taking my eyes off the doorway.

"Same place you took McCully and his wife," Mrs. Gunther answered. "Have them ready for more questioning when he gets there."

*Questioning?* My heart skipped and I dropped my head back against the wall weakly. *The Snake lied. My parents are still alive!*

Biting my lip in indecision, I looked at the door to the lab beside the garage. *Can I rescue Dr. Kestler and still follow them to my parents?* The only way I even had a chance to follow that truck would be to leave now and get my car from across the street. Even that was slim. I had to rescue Dr. Kestler first, and hope that delayed them enough for Matt to bring Chris.

169

# Jessica C. Joiner

Another quick glance assured me the men were still busy with their loading. Dashing across the broad opening, I paused on the other side to make sure Winston made it over safely. He did exactly as I had done and made it beside me without drawing attention to us. Perhaps he wasn't going to be as big a liability as I'd thought.

Relieved, I turned back to the slightly open door beside me. I listened carefully and peeked through the partly open door. To my right, I could see a heavy wooden desk covered with scattered papers held down by a glass paperweight. A long table full of assorted scientific equipment stretched across the back wall. Dr. Kestler, wearing a white lab coat, was working alone at this table with his back to the door. Quickly, I shoved the door open just enough for Winston and me to enter and closed it behind us.

"Dr. Kestler," I whispered urgently, crossing the room and laying my hand on the preoccupied scientist's shoulder.

Dr. Kestler jumped and turned to face us.

"Cadet McCully! What are you doing here? Who's your friend?" The surprise on Dr. Kestler's kindly face turned to worry. "Don't tell me they got you, too!"

"I've come to get you out of here," I answered, cutting Winston off as he opened his mouth to introduce himself. There wasn't time to explain the whole story. I guided Dr. Kestler to the door.

"How did you know where to find me?" Dr. Kestler looked puzzled. His eyes narrowed and he shifted

# A Tragic Introduction

his body between me and whatever he had been working on. "How much do you know about my experiment?"

"Enough to know we need to get out of here now." I stretched my arm across his back and pushed him more firmly to the exit.

Winston's eyes flicked nervously toward the door as if he expected someone to burst in at any time. Frankly, I was expecting the same thing. The uncertainty made me almost as nervous as Winston was acting.

"I'll answer any questions you want later," I promised, though I wasn't sure I had that many answers. "The Snake or his men will be here any minute."

"But I can't leave my invention in the hands of these madmen!" Dr. Kestler twisted away from me and started hastily scooping up his papers. "Do you know what they could do with it?"

"Yes." Just like I had a pretty good idea what they could do to us. "But it's probably already loaded on the truck. We have to leave without it."

"I won't leave it," Dr. Kestler said, his voice rising in protest. "Not again."

"Forget the stupid invention!" Winston shrilled back at him. So much for his keeping quiet. "They're going to kill us all if we don't get out of here."

"Not so loud," I said through clenched teeth. If anyone over heard the two of them… "You'll bring the guards. Then they *will* kill us all!"

"You're just as bad as your parents and those other agents SATURN sent to 'protect' me," Dr. Kestler shouted. He seemed to be concerned only for his invention, not at all for his own safety – or ours. "Always telling me what to do with my invention. It's mine, do you hear! And I…"

I clapped my hand over Dr. Kestler's mouth. Too late. Footsteps hurried toward the door. We wouldn't even have time to hide.

"Who do we have here?" Mrs. Gunther's voice was sugary as she and two other thugs entered the room.

Blowing out a frustrated breath, I put on a brave face as I turned toward them. Dr. Kestler gripped my arm with trembling hands. Winston scrambled to stand beside me and tried to put on a brave face as well. He just looked like he was in pain.

"I see you decided to come out of hiding after all." Mrs. Gunther pointed her gun at my chest. Winston took a small step away from me.

*Lord, give me courage.* I swallowed hard, forcing myself to look Mrs. Gunther in the eye instead of focusing on the gun. I had to stay strong if I wanted to rescue Dr. Kestler and Winston. *Don't let me get us all killed.*

"I told you he would eventually come here," Dr. Kestler spoke up. His voice no longer sounded gentle or soft. I closed my eyes and took a deep breath as I realized where I'd heard it before. *How could I have been fooled?*

"You were right, boss," Mrs. Gunther conceded and chuckled. "Like always."

Dr. Kestler's grip on my arm tighten like a vise. That's where I had heard the voice before; in the

# A Tragic Introduction

darkened room, coming from the shadow that had interrogated us.

Dr. Kestler was the Snake.

Fear stiffened my body as I glared at the evil grin that had transformed Dr. Kestler's normally pleasant face. He'd managed to fool SATURN and my parents as well.

Dr. Kestler laughed harshly at my reaction. "Surprised, Cadet McCully?"

"You brought us into a trap," Winston wailed at me. "We're going to die, and it's all your fault!"

At a gesture from Mrs. Gunther, one of the thugs grabbed him roughly by the arms as well. Winston's wails softened to whimpers, which stopped when Mrs. Gunther turned her gun to point at him.

*Why didn't I realize that Dr. Kestler was the Snake before now? Both Winston and I could have been safely outside with Matt and Trinity.* I quickly shook off the feelings of guilt Winston's accusations raised. Whether it was my fault or not, I was going to have to be the one to think of a way out. Winston was already too panicked to do any good.

*I have to stall Dr. Kestler until Chris gets here. Matt and Trinity are our only chance.*

"You're the Snake?" I knew I was just stating the obvious, but I was still too stunned to think of anything better.

Dr. Kestler laughed again. "SATURN never realized they were helping one of their most dangerous enemies create the ultimate weapon."

"But why?" I prodded, trying to think of a way to escape as Dr. Kestler talked. We might not have time to wait for SATURN. "Why would a terrorist want to work with SATURN?"

"Are you kidding? I had full access to SATURN's protection and funding. Plus, I rather enjoyed the irony of working right under their noses," Dr. Kestler said proudly. "And as Dr. Kestler, I had nearly unlimited access to the information at the facilities they kept me at."

"Then why wreck my parents' plane and stage the theft?" I asked. In his pride, Dr. Kestler seemed willing to give me the answers I needed. "It sounds like you had it made."

"Your parents suspected me. Mrs. Gunther planted a remote control device and the bomb in their plane and faked their deaths to keep them from telling anyone." Dr. Kestler explained. "The nerve gas was supposed to discourage any hope Agent Marshall had that they might be still alive. I could have just killed them, but they have information I need." His grip on my arm tightened painfully. "I staged the theft to get my invention away from SATURN and my own kidnapping to throw suspicion off myself. Mrs. Gunther suggested the envelope in her dresser as an added touch."

He smiled nastily at me. "I suspected SATURN sent you and Cadet Marshall to keep an eye on me. That's why I sent Mrs. Gunther to search your room. When she didn't find anything conclusive, I had her try to scare you off by running your car off the road."

"Why tell me my parents died?" I tried to yank my arm loose, but Dr. Kestler squeezed harder. I wasn't

## A Tragic Introduction

getting free of his iron grip. *Don't let him get tired of answering questions before Chris and Matt get here.*

"I had hoped to shake you up enough that you'd be willing talk when I questioned you later, but your friends escaped before I had a chance." Dr. Kestler was beginning to sound bored.

I tried to swallow my panic. If he got bored, he might decide to use us for his entertainment. "Where are my parents now?"

"Question and answer time is over. I believe you have stalled long enough." Dr. Kestler pulled a small pistol out of a pocket in his lab jacket, let go of my arm, and took a step back. I found myself looking directly into the barrel of his gun as he held it inches from my face. "SATURN will be here soon, and I can't afford your being alive to tell them what you know."

He grinned at me maliciously as his finger tightened on the trigger.

"Are you ready to die?"

# Chapter

I closed my eyes and bit my lip as I prepared for the impact of the bullet. Winston screamed, all pretense of bravery gone. There was no way out of this one. Chris and SATURN hadn't arrived; we hadn't been rescued at the last moment like in the movies. The verse Matt had quoted to me earlier came back ironically. *Though He slay me*... I really hadn't taken it that literally. I began to ask God to forgive my for anything I could remember ever doing wrong.

The crack of exploding gunpowder took my breath away. Winston let out another long, piercing shriek. I was sure I was dead.

# Jessica C. Joiner

My eyes flew open. It took me a whole second to realize that I wasn't dead. I hadn't been shot; the gunshot had come from somewhere down the hall. It took Dr. Kestler and his men two seconds to realize the same thing. That one second of distraction was all that I needed. I yanked the still screaming Winston from the thug's distracted grip and dragged him behind the large, solid wood desk sitting to my left. I crouched down next to him, holding him down so he couldn't try to stand in his panic. His screaming continued, but I couldn't risk using one hand to cover his mouth. Both of my hands were busy keeping him from getting up and running for the door. Besides, Dr. Kestler already knew where we were, it wasn't worth trying to cover Winston's mouth now.

"Gunther," Dr. Kestler shouted as the gunfire in the hall continued. "SATURN's here! Get out there and help the others stop them. I'll take care of these two."

I peeked cautiously around the edge of the desk to see Mrs. Gunther and the two thugs leave the room. I couldn't see Dr. Kestler without making myself a target. If I had to sit here holding Winston down, we may as well just surrender now. I shook him sharply and turned him to face me.

"Sit still and shut up," I snarled at him, giving him my most threatening look. "He'll shoot any part of your body that appears around this desk."

Winston stopped screaming and struggling. Relieved, I loosened my grip on him. Still shaking

178

# A Tragic Introduction

violently, he crawled under the desk and curled up tightly in the space normally reserved for a person's legs.

"You can't really believe that desk can protect you from me," Dr. Kestler sneered, his voice filled with hatred. My attention snapped back to him and the problem of escape. "Eventually, I will kill you."

Dr. Kestler's voice was slowly edging toward the desk, between the door and us. I wasn't going to be able to slip past him without getting shot, and I wouldn't leave Winston.

Dr. Kestler kept talking, but I stopped listening. I had to figure out a way to get rid of Dr. Kestler without getting killed. I remembered seeing the round glass paperweight on the desk. It had looked to be about the size of an orange. If I hit Dr. Kestler with it hard enough, I might be able to wrestle the gun from him while he was distracted. I rubbed my arm as I remembered the strength of his grip. He was stronger than he looked, but I was fairly sure I could take him.

*Right. I'd be more likely to get shot before I can even get to the paperweight.*

I shook off my pessimism. I was out of options. *We'll both be shot any way as soon as Dr. Kestler gets around the desk. Attempting to distract Dr. Kestler would give us a chance.*

Glancing at Winston to be sure he wasn't going anywhere, I slid my hand up to the desktop and felt for the paperweight. *Help me find find it before Dr. Kestler notices my hand crawling across the desk.*

Crack! Another gunshot echoed in the small room; this time followed by a sharp pain in my hand as

# Jessica C. Joiner

the bullet chewed into the wood desktop and sprayed splinters into my skin. I sat down hard, jerked my hand back down, and examined it critically. The splinters bled and stung, but at least it was only splinters and not a bullet. Bullet holes take a lot longer to heal than splinters. I imagine they also hurt a lot more.

Winston was screaming again and staring wide-eyed at my hand. I shook my head to reassure him, but his screaming just became more frantic. He was looking up at something else.

I followed Winston's gaze to a pair of shiny black shoes standing beside the desk. The shoes were connected to a pair of legs in black trousers covered by a white lab coat. My eyes followed the legs up to see Dr. Kestler looking down at us. My heart sank in despair. Dr. Kestler's gun was pointed down at us, too.

"Please don't kill me. Don't kill me!" Winston began to beg hoarsely. "Kill him, he's the super spy."

"I'll kill both of you right now if you don't shut up." Dr. Kestler pointed the gun at Winston just long enough to make his point and turned it back to me. His point was made; Winston drew himself into an even smaller ball and began to sob like a baby.

Part of me, a large part of me, wanted to crawl under the desk and join him. I forced myself to glare at Dr. Kestler defiantly.

"Perhaps I shouldn't kill you, Cadet McCully." The grin on his face looked like it would better suit a crocodile. "Perhaps I should take you with me. Maybe

## A Tragic Introduction

your parents would be more willing to talk if they thought it might save your life."

I caught my breath as I stared at the gun barrel facing me. It was close enough to my face that I could actually smell burnt gunpowder. SATURN was still exchanging shots with Dr. Kestler's men just outside the door, too busy to get to us in time.

If I gave up, Dr. Kestler would have me as a hostage to use against SATURN and my parents. If I resisted, Dr. Kestler would shoot me dead in seconds. Neither was a good option. I closed my eyes tightly and took a deep breath. I'd rather die now rather than let this maniac use me to torture my parents before killing me anyway. I might be able to keep him busy him long enough for SATURN at least to get Winston out of here. *Dr. Kestler's not taking me anywhere without a fight.*

Preparing to lunge at Dr. Kestler in one last reckless attempt to escape, I steeled my muscles. I never moved. A gunshot cracked from the doorway and drywall rained from the ceiling, but the desk kept me from seeing the gunman.

Muttering angrily, Dr. Kestler ducked past me and pushed a button under the edge of the table along the back wall. In a second, a section of the table slid aside and he was gone. I sat still for a moment, too relieved to be alive to even think about moving.

"Please Lord, please, don't let me be too late," Matt raised his terrified voice from the direction of the gunshot. "Scott? Are you all right? Please, answer me!"

"I'm fine." I stood slowly, flexing my sore hand. "You were right on time."

"I thought… I thought I was too late." Matt's normally tan face was deathly white and his eyes were wide with fear. He spoke softly, a catch in his voice. "I heard a gunshot and then Winston screaming. When I got in here, all I saw was Dr. Kestler with a smoking gun and one of your feet sticking out from behind the desk. I was sure…"

"Just a few scratches," I reassured him, not wanting to admit how close it had been. "But how did you get back in?" I was pretty sure Chris would never have agreed to let Matt come along.

"Chris left Trinity and me with an agent at the diner. He couldn't keep an eye on both of us. I slipped out the window of the men's room and back inside here. Chris and his men were too busy with their gunfight in the garage to see me slip by." Matt shrugged, a sheepish grin on his face. "The gun's been tucked in my waistband all along, I guess my tee-shirt covered it."

"Well, I'm certainly glad you're here." I glanced toward the hidden exit in the wall. "We need to go after Dr. Kestler."

"I'm staying right here." Winston's hoarse voice rose from beneath the desk. "If you want to offer yourselves as targets for that nutcase, fine, but leave me out!"

"Sit tight. SATURN will be in here soon enough." I was relieved he was finally willing to stay behind.

# A Tragic Introduction

"What's going on?" Matt tucked the smoking gun back in his waistband. "Why was Dr. Kestler trying to kill you?"

"He's really the Snake." I wiped the blood off my hand onto the leg of my jeans and ran my fingers under the worktable, feeling for the button that controlled the secret door. "And he's getting away."

My fingertips brushed a recess in the wood and I pressed hard. The secret entrance slid open again. This time Matt and I disappeared through it, leaving Winston to be rescued by SATURN.

The passage opened into a large garage. Three of the walls were lined with boxes and several expensive looking objects – including a rather strange looking invention. The wall to our left was taken up by a huge open door. Three very expensive-looking cars were parked in the middle of the room. Dr. Kestler sat in a shiny black sports car, the only hardtop in the group.

Matt and I ran to catch him before he back out, but we were too far away. Desperately, Matt fired twice at the car's tires.

"No way," I muttered as the shots buried themselves in the thick tires with a soft thunk. Matt's aim was surprisingly good, but the bullets didn't even slow the car down. "What's he driving? A tank?

The driver's door popped open for a moment, just long enough for Dr. Kestler to throw a shiny metal can at us. The can poured smoke into the garage.

"We'll never see him in this." Matt coughed as smoke filled the room. He fired two more shots blindly into the smoke.

"If we can get outside into the fresh air before he gets away, we might still catch him," I replied, plowing through the smoke toward the exit.

Walking through the smoke was like trying to walk in the dark, only worse. Darkness doesn't burn your eyes and throat. I kept my breathing shallow and pulled the collar of my tee shirt over my mouth and nose to avoid inhaling any more of the smoke than I had to.

Because I couldn't see, I strained my ears to catch the sound of Dr. Kestler's car. I didn't like what I heard. The purr of the sports car's eight-cylinder engine was heading the wrong way. A pair of hazy headlights flashed through the smoke, bearing down on us fast.

"Get out of the way!" I grabbed my unwitting friend, threw him aside, and dove down next to him. A breeze tugged at my feet as the car roared by.

"That was close." Matt coughed as he sat up. "I didn't even see him. Thanks, Scott."

"Call us even." I stared out the garage door as I sat up also. The smoke had cleared enough to see that the man responsible for my parents' disappearance was gone.

"Scott? Matt?"

I turned toward the door to the lab. Through the last wisps of smoke, I could see four men stepping through the passage I hadn't bothered to close. As they ran closer, I recognized Chris in the lead.

# A Tragic Introduction

"The Snake just drove off!" I called to him, pointing toward the exit. "He's driving a black sports car. He's really Dr. Kestler!"

If I had expected to surprise Chris, I was disappointed. He simply said a few words to the men with him and turned back to Matt and me. The three men returned to the lab.

"My men will set up a dragnet, but I doubt we'll catch him. The Snake's too slippery to be captured that way." Chris gave me an appraising look, his gaze pausing on my hand. "Are you all right?"

"Just some splinters," I assured him quickly. We had more important things to discuss. "Did you guys know that Dr. Kestler was the Snake all along?"

"Certainly not." Chris looked offended as he helped us to our feet. "If we had even suspected such a thing, we would have never let you two go near his house. I received word about an hour ago that our men had found evidence linking Dr. Kestler to the Snake. I was on my way to the diner to pull you two off the case when Matt called."

"That's why you weren't surprised when Scott told you who he was," Matt said, offering Chris the butt of the gun he was still holding.

"That's also why I was so upset when you told me on the phone that Scott had stayed behind to find Dr. Kestler." Chris took the gun, looking at it and then at his brother reproachfully. "You were supposed to stay behind at the diner with Trinity. I…" He paused awkwardly and looked at me. "Knowing what I did about Dr. Kestler, I really didn't expect to find you or Winston alive. I didn't want Matt here when we found you."

"I can't believe you actually expected me to stay behind." Matt's mouth curved crookedly. The fear in his eyes showed he still hadn't quite recovered from the fright he had gotten when he found me.

"I'm glad you didn't." I clapped him on the back. Now that all the excitement was over and I realized how close I had actually been to being killed, I felt a little dizzy. "Or Chris probably wouldn't have found us alive."

"We found Winston under the desk." Chris smirked wryly. "It took us quite a while to convince him that we were the good guys. I had one of the agents take him back to the diner."

"I'll bet he tried to take all the credit, once he realized who you were," Matt said derisively.

"He did," Chris confirmed, his grin widening, "but it's kind of hard to believe coming from a guy hiding under a desk."

Let Winston try to take the credit. We were alive. My *parents* were alive. That's all that mattered to me at the moment.

"Matt told me about Eric and Marisa," Chris said tightly. Fire lit his eyes and his fists clenched. "I'm sorry, Scott. I'll get the Snake for he did to them, I swear to you that I will."

# A Tragic Introduction

Matt had obviously only related to him the lies the Snake had told us, he didn't know the new information I had found.

"They're not dead." I stepped out in front of Chris and Matt just as we returned to the lab. "Dr. Kestler had them transported to another base for questioning."

"Scott, you can't keep denying…" Chris' voice held a note of warning, but his eyes darted away uncertainly.

"I'm serious. Dr. Kestler admitted to telling me they were dead to upset me into talking." I kind of left out the part where he also threatened to use me against them. "Mrs. Gunther knows where my parents are. Question her."

Chris looked at me thoughtfully before answering. Hope glittered in his eyes. "I will, Scott, personally. I'll let you know what we find out."

"If there's anything we can do to help…" I hinted, trying not to sound too eager.

Chris laughed. "It will be a long time before I'm willing to gamble on you two staying out of trouble. I already have to look forward to explaining to Mr. Jackson how I allowed you and your friends get captured by the Snake. I think we'll let SATURN take care of finding your parents and capturing Dr. Kestler."

"At least we got the invention back." Matt spoke up. "That might help calm Mr. Jackson down a little. The

Jessica C. Joiner

Snake's men were just finishing loading it onto their truck when we arrived."

"Come on." Chris turned to go. "We need to get back to the diner. Your friend Trinity probably thinks we're all dead by now."

188

# Chapter

As soon as we entered the diner, Trinity bolted up from the booth she had been sharing with Winston and a pair of SATURN agents and flung her arms around my neck. I stepped back in surprise as Winston glared at me. I could bet he didn't get a welcome like that when he arrived.

"Scott." Trinity sobbed and buried her tear-streaked face in my neck. "I was sure…"

She took a step back and looked at me, gasping when she saw the dried blood on my hand and the smear of blood on my jeans. "What happened?"

"Nothing." I rubbed my hand fiercely against my leg, embarrassed by her attention. "Just some splinters, that's all. I've been hurt worse in football practice."

Her hair brushed softly against my ear as she squeezed me tightly again. I looked desperately over her shoulder, hoping for Chris and Matt to rescue me one more time. They just grinned as if they were enjoying my discomfort.

"I thought I would never see you again," she whispered.

"God protected us." I pulled away from her and held her at arm's length. "Just like we asked him to."

"Your God had nothing to do with it," Winston snapped. "It was my appeal to that terrorist's mercy that saved us."

I glared at him angrily. It was one thing to try to take the credit from me, it was entirely another to try to take it from God.

"Cadet Daytona." Chris rolled his eyes. "If I were you, I would be careful about taking the glory from the One who made you. He might not be so willing to help you next time."

Winston crossed his arms, slid down in the booth, and fell silent, apparently not willing to argue with a secret agent.

Trinity gave Chris a thoughtful look, seeming impressed that even he believed in God. She turned back to me and nodded slowly. "I think I'd like to hear more about your God."

# A Tragic Introduction

I grinned at Matt. This was turning out to be a pretty good day after all. "Why don't you let me and Matt take you home? We can tell you all about Him on the way."

"You guys go back to school." Chris stepped forward and laid his hand on Matt's shoulder. "I'll be by sometime tomorrow to get your statements."

"You want to ride with us, Winston?" I faced the still glowering teen. I could feel both Matt and Trinity's eyes burning into my back. I ignored them. "You might learn something."

"If I want to learn about God, I'll go to my parents' church," He scoffed and rose to his feet. "Besides, I wouldn't dream of riding in your death trap, especially after what I've just been through. My car is parked down the street."

With that parting shot, he marched out the door and down the street. I wasn't too disappointed he'd declined my offer. I'd spent enough time with him today to last a lifetime.

After saying goodbye to Chris and the other SATURN agents, Matt, Trinity, and I left the diner and piled into my car. I opened the front passenger's door for Trinity and rounded the car to the driver's seat as Matt climbed in the back.

"I was really scared back there," Trinity admitted. Her blue eyes looked at me with a shadow of terror creeping back into them. "In the warehouse, I mean. I really thought that guy was going to kill us. I'm… I'm not ready to die."

# Jessica C. Joiner

"I know, Trinity, believe me." I pulled the car onto the road and shuddered as my mind replayed the fear I'd felt in the Snake's office. "I'm not really ready to die either, but at least I know that I would go to heaven if I did."

"I'd like to know that, too," Trinity said softly, her eyes moist. "Can you tell me how?"

I glanced back at Matt in the rear-view mirror. He folded his hands in front of him to indicate that he would be praying for me.

*Please, God, help me say the right words.*

"The Bible tells us there is only one way to heaven." I guess I'm not really good at being subtle. Besides, it was a pretty short trip back to the Academy. "That's by believing that Jesus Christ died to pay for our sins, was buried, and rose from the dead three days later."

"Why would Jesus *die* to pay for my sins?" Trinity asked doubtfully.

"Because He loves you." We were stopped at a red light, so I turned to look at her. "He wants you to be able to go to heaven with Him."

Trinity paused for a moment to digest the information. "You say he *rose from the dead?*"

"Jesus wasn't just any man." I returned my gaze to the road as the light turned green. "He was God come to earth as man. Not even death can defeat God."

"But what do I have to *do?*" Trinity asked. "There's got to be something I have to do to prove that I

## A Tragic Introduction

*deserve* to go to heaven. Is that why you guys go to church all the time?"

"No." I hurried to explain. We had already passed through the front gates of the Academy and were turning toward the faculty housing. Trinity lived in the last house on the left and I could see the picket fence surrounding it just up ahead. "Nothing we could do would be good enough for us to deserve heaven. Jesus paid for the penalty for our sin for us. He wants to give us heaven as a gift. All you need to do is accept it."

"Wow," Trinity said. Awe, uncertainty, and more than a little skepticism were packed into that one word. "That's a lot to think about. I guess I... well, I sort of expected you to tell me I needed to come to church with you guys and do nice things for people. I'm going to need time to think about what you said."

As I pulled into her driveway, I wanted to beg her not to wait, but I didn't want to pressure her to make a decision she wasn't ready for. Or worse, turn her off entirely. "When you're ready, you know where to find me."

"Thanks, Scott." She looked at me gratefully as she stood in the open car door. "You too, Matt. I'll see you guys on Monday."

Matt and I waved as Trinity closed the door and went into her house.

At Matt's insistence, I paid a quick visit to the nurse's station to get my hand taken care of before heading to our dorm. Winston was nowhere to be seen. If he was half as tired as I was, he probably went to bed as soon as he got back.

When we finally returned to our room, Matt and I changed our clothes and tossed our exhausted bodies into our beds.

My body may have been tired, but my mind wasn't so cooperative. I dreamed that I was on a picnic with my parents, just like one we had gone on last summer. The dream was so vivid and real I could hear the birds in the nearby trees and smell the freshly cut lawn and the fried chicken Mom had packed in the picnic basket. She spread a blue tablecloth on the ground and set out our lunch while Dad and I tossed a football nearby.

"Come on, you guys," Mom called to us. "Get your lunch before the ants do."

"Smells delicious, Marisa, like always." Dad kissed her forehead as he sat down beside her. He slipped his arm around her waist and pulled her closer to him.

"Eric." She pushed him away with a giggle. "Not in front of Scott!"

"Scott's a big boy now." Dad gave me sly smile and a wink. "He needs to see that his parents love each other very much."

I already knew how much my parents cared for each other, and right now my attention was on something else. A black sports car like the one the Snake had escaped in pulled into the grass behind my parents. Two thugs climbed out and circled the car. I opened my mouth to warn my parents, but no sound came out.

# A Tragic Introduction

The men grabbed my parents and yanked them to their feet, spilling the contents of the picnic basket all over the tablecloth. I tried to take a step forward to rescue them, but my feet were rooted to the spot. I screamed for the men to stop, for someone to help, but no sound escaped my lips. The thugs stuffed my parents into the back seat of the car and climbed in after them. As the car pulled away, my parents looked out the rear windshield at me, their eyes begging me to help them. I couldn't. I was helpless.

With a gasp, I sat upright in my bed. My clothes and hair were plastered to my body with sweat. My heart was pounding and I was breathing hard. The dream had seemed so real.

"You okay, Scott?" Matt murmured as he flipped on the lamp on the nightstand between our beds.

I swallowed hard and tried to steady my shaking hands. "Just a nightmare."

"About your parents?" Matt propped himself up on one elbow and looked at me sympathetically.

Confused, I looked at him. *How does he know I was dreaming about them?*

"You called for them just before you woke up," Matt explained.

"I dreamed we were at a picnic together when two men took them away. I couldn't do anything to help them." I paused and looked at Matt, clenching my fists with determination. "I'm going to find them, Matt. No matter what it takes, I *will* find them."

"You know," Matt said as he turned the light back off and rolled over in his bed, "I think I'm beginning to believe you."

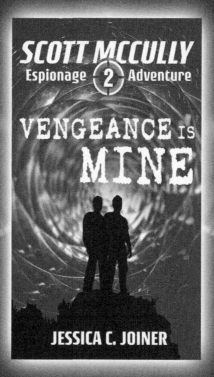

# Chapter

Beep! Beep! Beep! Bee…

An obnoxious alarm pierced into my sleep-fogged brain. I groaned and rolled over, jamming my pillow over my head to stifle the noise as my roommate, Matt Marshall, punched the snooze on his alarm clock for the second time that morning. 0630 came early enough without having to be wakened every nine minutes for the forty minutes before.

"Just one more snooze, Scott," Matt mumbled to me, more asleep than awake. He'd said that every time he hit the snooze. I knew better. He still had eighteen minutes before he was required to get up.

# Jessica C. Joiner

With another groan, I glanced at the clock sitting on the nightstand between our dorm room's twin beds. 0612. I closed my eyes and fell back onto the bed, my pillow in my hands. *Only two more alarms before Matt decides to get out of bed.*

I covered my head with the pillow again and tried to go back to sleep. "Too late now." With a grunt, I sat up and threw my covers off. I glanced around the room and tried to decide if the dawning sunlight coming through the window was enough to see to get dressed by.

*Not worth it,* I decided with a sigh. An unnoticed wrinkle in my uniform could get me in serious trouble when I went down for morning formation. The drill sergeant at John Jay Military Academy could be really particular about the student's uniforms. He was especially tough on seniors like Matt and me, who he regarded as having been at the military school long enough to know better.

Dropping my bare feet to the carpeted floor, I walked over to my desk, flicked on the desk lamp, and glanced apprehensively at my roommate. Matt rolled over in his bed, but showed no other sign of waking. I almost didn't care if I woke him or not, it was about time he got up anyway.

A stack of letters I hadn't had a chance to open the day before sat in the middle of my desk. Wednesdays could get really hectic between school and church and I hadn't had time to get to them. I had time now. I plopped down at my desk and picked up the three letters. I glanced at the first one before tearing it open. My name,

# A Tragic Introduction

Scott McCully, was written in my grandma's beautiful cursive on the front of the envelope. Shaking my head, I read the letter in spite of already knowing what it was going to say. My grandparents in Texas were offering to come get me for the third time in the two weeks since I'd told them my parents had disappeared. I'd already told them – twice – that I preferred to stay at the Academy. I wearily ran my fingers through my short, blond hair. I'd just have to tell them again.

The second letter was a voucher check from SATURN, the top-secret government agency my parents had worked for before they had disappeared. It was for the damages to my rusty old sedan while I was helping SATURN track down the terrorist responsible for my parents' disappearance. I smiled to myself. It was for more than the value of the car itself. I'd tried to tell Mr. Jackson that it would cost more to repair the damages to my worthless car than to replace it, but the head of SATURN had still insisted on covering the cost of the repairs.

*I suppose I could use the money to replace the car anyway.* I set the check aside. It would be better than paying to fix that old death trap.

The last letter was in a plain envelope with a printed label and no forwarding address. Curious, I tore it open and unfolded the short, typed letter inside. My eyes widened as I read - then reread - the contents.

Beep! Beep! Beep! Bee…

"Matt!" I hissed. "Shut that thing off and get over here!"

# Jessica C. Joiner

"I've still got nine minutes," Matt mumbled, pulling his blankets over his head.

I stood, flipped the switch for the room's overhead lights, and walked over to Matt's bed. The letter still clutched in my right hand, I used my left hand to yank Matt's covers off him.

"Catch up between classes." I ripped the pillow out of my friend's hands and stuffed the letter in his face.

"What's the big…" Matt began to protest, then gave a low whistle as he read the letter. "Where'd this come from?"

"It came in the mail yesterday." I sat down on the edge of Matt's bed . "I just opened it."

"'One by one, you and your friends will pay for what you did,'" Matt read aloud. He looked up at me, his brown eyes wide. "Is this for real?"

For an answer, I grimly pointed to a small, red drawing of a coiled rattlesnake in the lower right corner of the paper.

"The Snake!" Matt breathed, staring at the symbol used to identify the terrorist who had taken my parents.

"Apparently he wants to get back at us for stopping his plans to create the ultimate weapon."

"He kidnaps your parents, makes everyone believe they're dead, and tries to take over the world, and *he* wants revenge." Matt snorted derisively. "Go figure."

A burning ball of rage rose in my throat as I remembered the day over a month ago that had started the biggest nightmare of my life. My parents had canceled a visit with me again. I had been used to their unreliability

# A Tragic Introduction

and had not been worried, just a little disappointed. Until Matt's secret agent brother, Chris, came to tell me that my parents had been killed in a plane crash.

I had refused to accept the fact that they were dead. When SATURN, the agency Chris worked for, refused to give me any answers, I began to look for them myself.

The answers were not at all what I had anticipated. My parents weren't the average middle-class couple I thought they were. They were really spies for SATURN and their plane had been wrecked while they were protecting a revolutionary new weapon and its inventor, Dr. Isaac Kestler, from a terrorist known as the Snake. There were no bodies found in the wreckage, and I began to suspect that they had been kidnapped by the Snake.

With the help of my friends, I'd discovered that Dr. Kestler *was* the Snake. The three of us had helped retrieve the weapon and capture the Snake's men, but the terrorist escaped. With him escaped my chances of finding my parents. I was later able to convince SATURN that my parents were still alive, but they still hadn't found them. If the Snake truly wanted to get revenge on me, there'd be no easier way to get it than through my parents.

"Scott," Matt spoke up, interrupting my thoughts. He was sitting up in his bed, looking at me with concern. "Worrying about your parents won't find them faster. Call Chris, maybe this letter will give them a lead."

"Good idea." I collected my thoughts and stood. "I'll call him now, then get ready for class." I picked up the receiver of the phone on the nightstand and dialed the number I'd now memorized from frequent use: Agent Christopher Marshall's cell phone.

"Agent Marshall," Chris's crisp voice rang clearly over the line. It sounded like he'd been up for a while.

"This is Scott." I took the letter back from Matt and looked it over as I spoke. "I got a letter I think you should see." I read it into the phone. "It's signed with a red rattlesnake."

There was a long pause on the other end of the line before Chris responded. "I'll be by this afternoon to get it. Have it and the envelope it came in ready for me about 1600. It could give us a lead to Kestler."

"And my parents," I added, even though it wasn't necessary. My dad had been Chris's mentor and I knew he was almost as eager to find them as I was. *Almost.*

"Lord willing," Chris agreed seriously. "We'll talk about getting protection for you guys when I get there. Until then, be careful."

"Right, see you then." I hung up the phone and turned back to Matt. "Chris will be here at 1600. He's coming for the letter and to discuss our protection here."

"I'm not so much concerned about protection here as I am about protection when I leave the campus," Matt commented as he began to dress for class. "I don't want to be trapped here until they catch that guy."

"Me neither." I pulled my sheets tight over my bed. "One of the reasons I'm still here at JJMA is so that

# A Tragic Introduction

I can continue to look for my parents. I can't do that if I'm confined to campus."

We dressed quickly and meticulously, pausing for a few moments to read our Bibles before heading to the cafeteria for breakfast.

After speeding through breakfast, we headed to the parade grounds for morning formation and drills. At 0900, we headed back to the Nathan Hale Administration Building for our first class - physics. We entered our classroom and took our usual desks beside each other about halfway to the front.

"Look on the bright side, Scott." Matt grinned as he took his textbook from his backpack and laid it on his desk. "At least our physics grades are up."

I smiled tightly before answering. We had gotten tutored by Dr. Kestler as part of the plan to help locate my parents. The tutoring really had helped; I was actually beginning to understand what Professor Davidson was saying. "I guess anyone who could invent a weapon that could take over the world ought to be able to tutor a couple of high school seniors in physics."

"Are you two talking about that awful scientist again?" Trinity Shiloh, a pretty, redheaded junior, dropped her books on the desk in front of mine. "He's not back around, is he?"

*Do I really need to get her involved?* I looked at Matt quickly before motioning for Trinity to come closer. She was already involved and the threat likely included her. I took the letter from my pocket and handed it to her to read.

# Jessica C. Joiner

"That's terrible." Her face went pale as she read. "Have you called Chris?"

"I have," I answered softly so the other students filling the classroom couldn't overhear. "He's coming over this afternoon. Until then, I just want to warn you to be careful. You were with us that day, too."

"Are you worried about me, Scott?" Trinity asked, a teasing glint in her blue eyes.

"Sure, I'm worried about you." I blushed slightly and tried to recover quickly. "You're my friend, aren't you?"

"Only a friend?" Matt ribbed, a huge grin on his face.

I shot him a look and was about to reply, when a cry from Trinity stopped me.

"Let go, you bully!"

Winston Datona III, JJMA's newest bully, yanked the letter out of Trinity's hand. She tried to grab it back from him, but he held it behind him just out of her reach.

"I saw you three standing around, and I needed to find out what all the commotion was about." Winston sneered condescendingly as he began to read. "I thought you might need my help."

The last time Winston wanted to "help", he got himself kidnapped with the rest of us. He ended up cowering under a desk in fear. Some help!

"We need you like a visit to the Superintendent's office," Matt snapped angrily.

# A Tragic Introduction

"Give the note to me, Winston," I said firmly, standing to my feet. I was several inches taller than Winston and wanted to use that to my advantage.

"So this is your letter, Spy Boy," Winston taunted. "Getting kidnapped by a terrorist once wasn't good enough, so you had to make up a new threat?"

"The note's real," Matt growled, coming up next to me. "And it's evidence. Give it back, or I'll get Superintendent Hinkly."

"Maybe I want to investigate for myself." Winston glared back, a challenge in his brown eyes. "Or are you afraid I'll get all the glory?"

"Give me that letter or I'll…" Matt took a step toward the smaller boy. He flexed his thick biceps threateningly.

"What's going on here?" an angry voice boomed behind us.

"Professor Davidson, sir." Winston smiled sweetly. "Cadets McCully and Marshall lost an important piece of paper. They were getting really upset about losing it, but I was able to find it for them and was just giving it back."

He handed the note back to the still seething Matt.

"Very good, then." Professor Davidson nodded, apparently satisfied by Winston's explanation. "Please take your seats, I'm about to call roll."

Winston's smile turned triumphant as he followed Professor Davidson and sat down on the front row.

"What a pain," Matt whispered to me as he sat down in his seat.

I nodded sympathetically. "Don't let him get to you. If he can make you lose your temper, he's won."

"I know." Matt sighed. "But he's so annoying."

"Attention, class," Professor Davidson called, tapping his ruler on the podium. "I want to introduce you to a new student here at JJMA. His name is Cadet Eugene Rogers."

Matt and I looked up to see a small blond teen with pale blue eyes and large glasses standing next to Professor Davidson. He looked down and traced a floor tile with his foot.

"Cadet Rogers is a junior this year," Professor Davidson continued. "I expect you all to make him feel welcome and to show him the ropes."

Professor Davidson scanned the class, his gaze passing over me and resting on Winston. "Cadet Daytona, I'm assigning you to give Cadet Rogers a tour of the campus and make sure he gets to all his classes today." Professor Davidson motioned to an empty desk next to Winston. "Cadet Rogers, you can sit here beside Winston."

"Scott!" Matt hissed, leaning across the aisle. "We need to rescue that poor guy before Winston torments him."

"We will," I assured him softly, "as soon as we can."

As soon as the class was dismissed, Winston led Eugene out of the classroom, looking for all the world

# A Tragic Introduction

like his best friend. Matt, Trinity, and I quickly tried to catch up.

When we finally reached Winston, Eugene was nowhere to be seen.

"Where's Eugene?" I glared at Winston's crooked grin suspiciously.

"He asked me where to find a restroom." Winston pointed his thumb behind him. "I showed him one."

"That's the ladies room," Matt cried angrily. "The men's room is the other direction!"

# ABOUT THE
# AUTHOR

## JESSICA C. JOINER

*IS A STAY-AT-HOME-MOM AND VOLUNTEER TEACHER WITH SIX KIDS, ONE CAT, AND ONE HUSBAND. SHE LOVES COMIC BOOKS, CLASSIC TV, AND WRITING FICTION.*

*READ MORE AT*
**AUTHORJESSICAJOINER**.*WEEBLY.COM*

If you like this book, please give me a good review.
On Amazon: amazon.com/author/jcjauthor
On GoodReads:
https://www.goodreads.com/JCJAuthor


Visit my website:
https://authorjessicajoiner.weebly.com

Follow me on Facebook: Author Jessica C. Joiner @JCJAuthor

Follow me on Twitter: @JCJAuthor

Follow me on Pinterest: Author Jessica C. Joiner

Made in the USA
Coppell, TX
04 June 2022

78460305R00125